# This Little Piggy Wound Up Dead

A Willow Crier Cozy Mystery

Book 3

Lilly York

# This Little Piggy Wound Up Dead

A Willow Crier Cozy Mystery

**Book 3**

©2016 by Lilly York

www.lillyyork.com

All rights reserved.

This book or parts thereof may not be reproduced in any form, stored in a retrieval system, or transmitted in any form by any means without prior written permission of the author or publisher, except as provided by United States of America copyright law.

Cover Design: Jonna Feavel
40daygraphics.com

Illustrations: Ben Gerhards

Interior Layout: Daniel Mawhinney
40daypublishing.com

Published by: Wide Awake Books
wideawakebooks.com

Also available in eBook publication

The following is a work of fiction. Names, characters, places, and incidents are fictitious or used fictitiously. Any resemblance to real persons, living or dead, to factual events or to businesses is coincidental and unintentional.

**Printed in the United States of America**

# Get your free short story!

## Grandpa Goes Missing

Find out what happened to bring Willow down to Oklahoma in the first place.

FREE short story only available here!

**www.lillyyork.com/shortstory**

*Get yours today!*

# Chapter 1

Willow woke to a crash and sat straight up. The dog was whining and pressed up against her. "Some guard dog you are." She heard the little pings of water hitting her bedroom window. The next rumble of thunder gave her an excellent reason to snuggle deeper down in her covers and keep her eyes closed. She loved sleeping to the sound of rain. In her opinion, there was no better sleeping conditions. She pat the dog's head. "It's just thunder, Clover. Nothing to worry about."

She was in that place, in-between consciousness and dreamland when a silent alarm started ringing in her head. It grew louder and as hard as she tried to shut the alarm off, it wouldn't go away. It was an alarm of concern, of something she was forgetting and needed to address.

Her eyes opened and she left the warmth of her cocoon and stood by her bedroom window. "It's raining. So what?" She asked out loud.

Then it hit her. The BBQ cook off. It was rain or shine.

## This Little Piggy Wound Up Dead

Clover was whining at her feet. "All right, girl. I'll let you out." She opened the back door and the dog hung out on the patio, looking frightened. "Clover, go on, go potty." Clover just stared at her. "Oh good grief. Are you kidding me?" She ran out into the back yard with the dog. "Now go potty! Why do both of us have to get wet?" Clover did her thing then ran for the door.

Willow toweled both of them off on the patio then made her way inside. Everything had been packed up the night before, well, except her duffle bag. She still had a few things to stuff in there. Now, she would need ponchos and a few umbrellas. The show must go on.

A few minutes later Embry padded through her front door, complaining as she did so. "I don't know why I had to drive all the way out here in the rain when I just have to turn around and go back."

"To help pack the truck."

She grumbled, then asked, "Mom, did you grab the hats I bought?"

"Already got 'em. They're sitting on the counter in the kitchen." Willow popped her head out of the bedroom door with her hat already perched on her head. The pink hats with a pig's face and piggy ears were perfect for their first bbq cook off. "I'm almost ready. Has Steve shown up yet?"

"He just pulled in. Looks like he has the smoker and the grill in the back of his truck. Should I have him put the coolers in there too?"

"Yeah, that'll work." Willow zipped up her duffle bag and set it by the front door. "I think that's it."

She watched as Steve hoisted the heavy cooler into the back of his truck bed. He had a small pull behind camper hooked up for Willow and Embry to use. He said he would be fine in the bench seat of his truck.

Willow was excited. This was her first bbq cook off. It was the real deal. She had all four required meats in the cooler; brisket, butt, ribs, and chicken.

She had read all about last year's winner, in fact, the team that won last year had won the past five years straight. They were certainly the team to beat. She wasn't fooling herself into thinking she could win this year, but, participating was the first step toward eventually winning. Maybe, just maybe, the champions would agree to mentor her. She could only hope.

She walked out and handed Steve his hat.

"Pink, huh?"

She grinned. "Do you have a problem with that?"

"Of course not." He grinned. "Real men wear pink." He placed the hat on his head and oinked in her direction. "Do you have more that needs loading?"

"Nope, I think this about does it." She tossed her duffle bag into the back of her Jeep. "Everyone ready?"

The Three Little Pigs caravan pulled into the park just after noon. Willow hopped out of her Jeep and opened an umbrella as she landed then told Steve she was going to check in and figure out where they were supposed to set up.

She returned with a map, and a few minutes later the three of them were busy setting up. Getting wet in the process.

Willow looked around the park, totally in her element. The smell of smoking meat was driving her crazy. Her stomach rumbled. She decided to take a quick walk and meet a few of the other participants. She wandered from camp to camp, introducing herself and pointing back toward her own camp, telling people to stop by anytime.

Almost everyone was friendly and welcoming. Some were even helpful, giving tips for her first bbq competition.

Her feet made squishing sounds with each step she took. Her rain soaked tennis shoes were going to be useless. The only other shoes she brought was a pair of flip flops. She leaned up against a big tree and proceeded to kick them off. Angry voices carried as the rain reduced to a drizzle.

"Bridget, I told you to stop talking to him. You're flirting and I won't have it."

"Dean, you don't own me. There's no ring on this finger."

"Own you? Yeah, I do and you know it. Don't you ever think otherwise."

She heard the unmistakable sound of a slap followed by Bridget angrily saying, "You're such a pig, do you know that?"

She saw the back side of Bridget as she stomped back to her camp. She peeked around the other side of the tree to find Dean still cradling his cheek. He started after her. Neither of them noticed Willow.

When Willow returned to camp, she hung her tennis shoes up to dry inside the camper and slipped on her flip flops. The smoker was ready to roll so she prepared her brisket and butt with her

## This Little Piggy Wound Up Dead

seasonings and secured them in the smoker. "Well, for now, that's that. Anyone want to get a bite to eat? We'll need to take turns babysitting."

Embry yawned. "Why don't you two run and get something. Bring me back a sandwich. I'm going to take a nap so I'll be ready for my shift." She held up her phone. "I'll set my alarm. No worries."

Embry crawled in to the readied camper and left Willow and Steve standing in the rain.

Steve watched the door shut firmly behind her. "Well, I guess she has it all figured out."

Willow smiled. "She usually does."

Steve and Willow sat down under a shelter with plates of pulled pork sandwiches, potato salad, and baked beans.

"This rain is giving me the chills." She zipped up her sweat shirt. A voice coming from the table next to theirs captured her attention.

She lowered her voice and told Steve what she had heard earlier when she was out walking.

"Hey, we aren't going to have any trouble this weekend. Not with our equipment, not with our neighbors, and certainly not with a pig. I'm off duty. So are you."

She distractedly nodded in agreement. "Do you think that young man she is talking to is the man Dean warned her off from?"

# Lilly York

"You didn't hear a word I said, did you?"

"Yes, I did. I was just wondering is all. I can wonder, can't I?"

Steve shook his head. "No, you are banned from wondering. You cannot wonder until you arrive home tomorrow evening."

She grimaced then took a bite of her sandwich.

Early the next morning, Willow crawled out of her bunk and stretched. She smelled coffee. Someone somewhere already had the stuff brewing. It was still dark out. She listened intently. She heard a few hushed voices, a dog barking, a jet ascending, but she didn't hear the pitter patter of rain. She felt the inside of her shoes. Still damp. She had 10 minutes until her turn with the smoker. She had to find a bathroom and coffee. And she had to hurry if she didn't want Embry upset with her. The girl was downright ornery when she was tired. Hunger made things 10 times worse.

Willow was nearly on top of Dean's camp when a rather behemoth of a man erupted. "I trusted him to keep this thing going. It was his only job. It's not even hot anymore." He turned on the spotlights he had set up around his very large smoker and gathered enough supplies to hopefully get his smoker up and running again. He opened it just as Willow was close enough to hear a string of expletives pour out of the man's mouth. He slammed it shut and stepped back as though his eyebrows, nose hairs, and chest hairs had all ignited. His smooth bald head was gleaming in the moonlight. The moonlight in direct competition with the startled whites of the man's eyes.

He began speaking in stuttered syllables. Willow stepped closer, trying to understand what the man was saying. He kept pointing to the smoker. His eyes danced back and forth between her and the closed unit. She finally had enough with the foreign tourist act and opened the smoker. She stared for a brief moment. Inside was a man, positioned with all fours bent, an apple in his mouth, and slowly rotating on the rotisserie. He'd been tied, not skewered. Thankfully.

"Oh goodness. It's the pig!"

# Chapter 2

Willow was getting awfully close to dancing. No one wanted to see a woman in her 40's dance. At least not in the way she was dancing. A small crowd was gathering so she found the big bald guy and let him know she'd be back.

The entire time Willow wiggled toward the bathroom, she found herself thinking about Mr. Pig in the smoker. She chastised herself. Dean. She would have to start calling him by his name. She doubted calling a dead man Mr. Pig was respectful. Even if his deserving it was questionable.

She did her business, with no leaks mind you, and hurried back to the scene of the crime. Steve was already examining the scene when she approached.

"Willow, there you are. I thought you'd be smack dab in the middle of..." He was interrupted by the big bald guy vying for Willow's attention.

"Oh good, you're back. I need you to give your, er..." He looked to Steve, knowing Steve already flashed his badge. "...statement to the other police."

## This Little Piggy Wound Up Dead

Willow shrugged her shoulders at Steve then followed the guy to the local police officers who were already on the scene.

Steve followed close behind, whispering to her as they walked. "Why do you need to give your statement?"

"Because I was walking by the camp when he opened the smoker and found the body. I saw the whole thing."

He rolled his eyes and looked heavenward. "Of course she did."

"If the bathroom in the trailer worked, I wouldn't be in this position."

"Oh sure, blame it on the bathroom."

She laughed. "I'm not blaming it on the bathroom, I'm blaming it on you."

Tired of calling the big bald guy, Big Bald Guy, she asked "What is your name?"

He stuck out his hand. "Preston Mosely. Nice to make your acquaintance, Ma'am."

"Nice to meet you too, Preston. Although I wish it were under more pleasant circumstances." She turned her attention back to Steve. "Now, I was walking by Mr. Mosely's camp…"

"Ma'am, call me, Preston."

She corrected herself. "I was walking by Preston's camp when he noticed his smoker was no longer smoking. He opened it up and jumped back. He was so upset, I decided to find out what had caused this big burly man to jump like a jack rabbit and that is when I found Dean, all propped up like a pig on a spit, apple in his mouth, the whole works. I called 911 and then had to hurry to the bathroom." She gave him a look. "I was just coming back from that trip when I ran into you. That's it. That's all I've got." She added for good measure. "And it's all I'm gonna have too. I have chicken and ribs that need tending back at our own camp. I can't be attaching myself to some murder case. Not again."

With that, she sat down at the picnic table to give her statement to the detective. She had no choice but to tell him about the argument she'd heard earlier between Dean and Bridget. Besides being present when the body was found, she really didn't think she had been much help.

Willow started back for her camp. The eastern sky was just beginning to lighten up. She was staring at the glowing horizon when she suddenly found herself face to face with Preston.

"Well, hello again."

He grinned. "Hello, Ma'am. Thank you for talking to the police. Dean may have been a bit of a trouble maker, but he was my nephew and I loved him. This is gonna kill my sister." He shook his head. "Would someone really go to these lengths to keep us from winning the contest again?"

Willow somehow doubted Preston sought her out to thank her. His grin seemed permanently glued to his face.

"It's hard to say what people will do. Almost anything it seems when they want something bad enough."

"I tell you the first people the cops should look at. The people who win the grand prize. They did it. I know it." He nodded then added. "Looks like I'm not needed at my camp now." He had the decency to turn a slight shade of pink. "I could help at yours, if you'd like. I did win the championship last year, in fact, five years running. You never know. We could be quite the team." He narrowed his eyes just a bit and the corners of his mouth turned ever so slightly upward.

Willow opened her mouth then closed it, then repeated. Just as she formulated a reply, Steve jogged up next to her.

"Oh, hey, Preston, right?"

Steve's voice sounded friendly. His face however…"The police are looking for you."

"Oh, okay. Thanks for letting me know." He turned to Willow. "And that offer still stands. I'll stop by your camp after I finish up."

Steve watched as Preston thundered away. "What was all that about? I think our competitor has a crush on you."

This time she was the one turning red. "Oh, he just volunteered to join our team, or at least to give us some help since he no longer has a team of his own."

"Did you agree?"

"No, not without talking to the rest of my team." She grinned. "You know, it might not be a bad idea to get some ideas from last year's winner. I had been hoping to get the winning team to mentor us. Looks like we could have just that."

He made some unintelligible grunt then changed the subject. "Did you happen to notice those strange marks on the victims face? And the lack of blood in the smoker?"

She nodded. "Yeah, I've been thinking about that. It looks like someone was stomping on his face and he definitely bled out somewhere besides that smoker." She glanced around the park. "It's got to be around here somewhere. I see the police are searching the park. I guess they are thinking along those same lines." Police officers were spread out over the park grounds, looking for the original crime scene.

"I knew you wouldn't be able to leave the investigation alone."

## This Little Piggy Wound Up Dead

She chose to ignore him. "And what do you think made those distinctive marks on his face? Those aren't from a normal shoe and certainly not a bare foot."

Steve grinned. No way would she be able to just leave this thing alone. "I don't know. I think we need to know more about our victim. Thankfully the local police are accepting my help. I'll see what I can find out. Do you think you and Embry can handle getting the chicken and ribs on without me?"

"You bet."

Willow and Steve parted ways. As Willow drew closer to their camp, she noticed Embry talking with someone although she couldn't quite tell who it was.

Embry raised her hand and waved hello just as Bridget turned and gave her a look that could singe the hair off even the hairiest little pig. Willow had to wonder if Dean had ever received one of those looks.

Willow approached the camp with trepidation. Embry widened her eyes to let Willow know she was in trouble.

"Hi, Bridget, right?"

"You know who I am. You had no problem ratting me out to the cops. I'm here to tell you to mind your own business."

Willow took a step backward. "I had to tell them what I heard. They have to explore every possibility. Besides, wouldn't it be nice to be crossed off the suspect list right away?"

She took a step closer, hands on her hips. "You ain't got no dog in this fight and how do you know my name should be crossed off that list?" She took yet another step closer.

Willow was certain she could feel the heat emanating from the young woman and took a step backward. "I just assumed."

A loud whistle blasted through the park and police officers started jogging in the direction it came from.

"Isn't that close to where you were arguing with Dean yesterday?"

Bridget's face showed alarm. "You just keep your nose where it belongs or I'll jerk a knot in your tail." She quickly walked away, toward her camp.

Embry and Willow watched her retreating back then turned to one another and both said, "A knot in your tail?" They busted out laughing.

# Chapter 3

Willow looked toward the gathering police officers with yearning.

"Mom, why don't you go? I'll finish up here."

She looked from the chicken to the ribs then to Embry. "I can help get these on the smoker. Then I'll go."

She applied the dry rub to the chickens while Embry applied rib rub. They would just have enough time to cook before the plating began. Willow was surprised the contest was moving forward with the murder and all. Then again she reasoned there might be a dual purpose in keeping the cook-off going. People would be less likely to leave before a new bbq king—or queen—was announced.

Police officers were busy getting information from contest participants. As long as everyone's basic information checked out, they could leave after the contest was over.

She had given her statement earlier. Embry still had to go and be questioned. "Why don't you run over to the pavilion and give your statement. After that, I'll head over to the crime scene."

Willow tucked the chickens and the ribs in the smoker then tested the brisket. She readied the serving containers with lettuce, parsley, and small containers of barbecue sauce.

After putting coffee on the fire, she put some bacon on to fry while she mixed a dozen eggs in a bowl with garlic, salt, pepper, and a dash of hot sauce. "Even crime solvers have to eat." The scent of cooking food caused her stomach to growl. "Yeah, I know. I'm working on it."

She had breakfast finished by the time Embry returned with Steve walking alongside her. She set the food on their folding table and poured some fresh coffee from the pot.

"Mom, you cooked. I'm starving."

All three of them quickly ate. Embry was still down a sleep shift so she stole away to her bunk. Steve and Willow talked murder.

"I take it they found the scene of the crime?"

Steve nodded. "Yeah, looks like someone killed him then moved his body to the smoker. Wonder what kind of statement they were trying to make."

## This Little Piggy Wound Up Dead

"Probably the obvious. That he was a pig." She put the dirty dishes in the dish pan to soak while Steve sipped his coffee.

He cleared his throat, then said, "Um, we have a favor to ask of you."

She looked up. "We?"

"Yeah, the metro police and myself." He continued. "Would you mind cozying up to Preston, Dean's uncle? He's not being very cooperative and well, he seems to have taken quite a shine to you."

"Do you mean Preston is being uncooperative with the police? Could be he has something to hide."

"That did cross our minds. Will you do it?"

She grinned. She knew Steve did not like Preston. Nothing personal, of course. He was just getting a little too close for comfort. She couldn't believe asking her was an easy thing for him to do. "I can do that. What are they suggesting? Going on a date with him?"

"Oh, no, that won't be necessary. Just talk to him. Maybe have a cup of coffee at the pavilion. See if you can get him to open up about Dean. That's all. Nothing more."

Willow laughed. "Oh, okay. I'll go see him. After you show me the crime scene."

He held his hand out for her to lead the way.

Willow walked outside the yellow crime scene tape, looking for anything out of the ordinary. Besides the red stain on the green grass, everything nearly looked normal. Nearly.

"Steve, look at that patch of dirt. Are you seeing what I'm seeing?"

Steve knelt down. The dirt had those distinctive marks in it. The same as Dean's face. "Some of these are deeper than others. I think we're looking for more than one person. They all seem to be wearing the same kind of shoe."

# Chapter 4

Willow smiled at the big bulky guy sitting across from her then sipped her coffee. She hated flirting, especially with someone she had no intention of trying to get to know. Besides, it felt conniving and manipulative. Two things she had no interest in becoming. She went for the straight forward approach. "Tell me about Dean."

Preston shrugged then sighed. "What do you want to know?"

"Well, tell me about him. His likes, his dislikes, his dreams and aspirations. His habits, both good and bad, his short comings. Tell me all about him. I want to feel like I really knew him."

Preston looked as though he was considering what to say. More importantly, what not to say. "My sister did the best she could with the boy." He tipped his cup. "Still, nothing much worked. He was destined for trouble."

"How do you mean?"

"She tried everything. Even had me take him on for a year or so, thinkin' he needed a strong male role model. He just never took to bein' the good Southern mama's boy the South is known for producin'."

"I've noticed there are a lot of gentlemen in the South."

"There sure are. Our mamas wouldn't have it any other way."

"When you talk about trouble, what kind of trouble did he get himself into?"

"Oh, let's see. He has a youngin'. Not that Dean had much to do with the little guy. 'Bout three years old now, I reckon."

"Is he still in a relationship with the little boy's mom?"

"No. As soon as he found out she was pregnant he hightailed it outta there." Preston stroked his beard. "He had real talent playin' baseball. Everyone said he was headed for the big time. Then he got mixed up in drugs and drinkin' and he lost his scholarship. The judge gave him a real good deal though. He had to coach a local team of bad boys. It was his way of making sure Dean used his talent to make a difference, or so he hoped."

"You mean Dean has been working with kids who have gotten in trouble? Teaching them how to play baseball?"

"Yeah, but he hadn't committed like he should have. Sometimes he would show up, sometimes not. Depended on what else he had going on. The kids would be knocking at the door, wondering where he was. Even had some local businesses that sponsored the team, bought them uniforms, shoes, the whole nine yards. If I'm remembering right, Dean was called to go back before the judge. Not sure what happened. I'd have to ask my sister."

"Who do you think killed him?"

Preston shook his head. "I don't know. Could be a drug dealer, some girl's jealous boyfriend, shoot—even the mad girlfriend. He's made a lot of people mad. Even me."

Willow tilted her head. "You? What did he do to you?"

"He drained my checking account. All 52,233 dollars. I was saving to get my own food truck. Had it all planned out. Guess I gotta start over or give up. Haven't decided yet."

"Any idea what he did with the money?"

"An idea or a guess? With Dean, I could guess he bought stock in monkey toothbrushes and anyone who knew him wouldn't even give it a second thought. If he wasn't spending his money on drugs, he was always into some get rich quick scheme."

"What did he do for a living?"

"He waited tables at Chilis."

"That's a long way from playing professional baseball."

"You're telling me. Some of the guys that were on his team are playing for the semi-pro team here in Oklahoma City. They could tell you more about his baseball playing days. A few of the guys have a camp a couple of rows over. They may have known him. If not, ask them where you can find Brian Wilson. Brian was also on the team and Dean's best friend. Kind of a jerk, but hey, so was Dean. And maybe you should talk with the guys he was coaching. They're a tough lot. Be careful."

Willow nodded her consent. So many people who had something against Dean. Why couldn't this one be a cut and dried mugging? Wouldn't that make things so much easier?

Before Willow knew what was happening, Preston was standing before her singing for all the world to hear. Not that she could understand a word of it. Apparently the man liked opera. She endured one song then quickly retreated while onlookers clapped heartily.

Willow ran through the information she had thus far. Bridget was somewhat of a mystery she had to get to the bottom of. She found out Bridget was a nurse at one of the local hospitals. She sure would like to question her co-workers but she highly doubted she would be able to talk Janie, or Embry for that matter, into going with her. Not after her last hospital fiasco. She'd have to do it on her own. She also made a mental note to talk to the members of both baseball teams. Perhaps they would know something useful. And then there was Brian. Sounded like they may have gotten into trouble together. He may be one to talk to. Unfortunately, even with the ever growing list of possible suspects, Preston was number one in her book. A person doesn't just give up 50,000 dollars and walk away peacefully. At least not in her experience. Willow turned and looked over her shoulder as Preston bowed before the crowd. Maybe the opera wasn't the only tragic story he's familiar with.

# Chapter 5

Willow adjusted her pink piggy cap and climbed the few stairs to the make shift stage. In spite of the dried out chicken and ribs, which Willow took full responsibility for ignoring the smoker during her shift, their team managed to get a runner's up ribbon for their brisket and butt.

From somewhere in the crowd, a loud, belting voice started singing something in Italian. Another opera song. He certainly looked the part but where does an Italian barbecue opera singing food truck wanna-be come from? And how in the world did she get lucky enough to have him fall for her?

With a red face, she descended the stairs. Steve was having a hard time keeping the smile off his face. Embry didn't even try. She was choking on her soda from laughing so hard.

Her serenading love interest was now standing before her.

"Sei la mia rosa."

Willow just stared. All her life she imagined having a good looking Italian whisper sweet nothings to her, the lull of the accent, the dark hair, the…southern accent mixed in? No way. She would never see the romance of the Italian language again, ever. Period. He ruined it. "I gotta go."

She nearly ran for their camp and began to tear down.

Embry and Steve followed close behind.

"Mom, that was priceless. Freaking awesome. I recorded the whole thing and put it on Facebook."

Willow came to an abrupt halt. "You did what? Take it down. I mean it, Embry. Take it down."

Embry fiddled with her phone. "I'll take it down, I promise. But, it'll have to be when I get home. I don't have a good enough connection to sign in."

She was just serenaded by an opera-singing Southern boy in front of at least a thousand people. Now her daughter put it on Facebook. *When will this day end?*

A war raged within Willow. One side was thrilled someone took the time to serenade her. The other side wished Steve had been the one to do so. Even though she knew he wasn't the type. Not for that kind of public display. Wasn't his nature.

Their small caravan headed toward home, Steve led the way, Willow and Embry followed.

"You're awfully quiet." Embry's voice sliced through the quiet.

Willow glanced at her daughter as she drove. The sun was setting and her eyes were hiding behind sunglasses. Her daughter was beautiful. Both inside and out. She had her whole life to live, dreams to chase, love to find, happiness to pursue. Willow didn't want to speak of time lost and days gone by. Yet, who would warn her daughter if not her?

Embry mistook her mother's silence for being upset. "Mom, I'm sorry I posted the opera love scene. Really, I am."

"Oh honey, you know I'm not upset about that. I just, well, I have a lot on my mind."

"Let me guess. A certain someone driving the car in front of us?"

"Am I that obvious?"

"To me, yeah. I don't think to him."

"That's good. One minute, he's acting jealous. The next, he's laughing that some guy is singing Italian love songs to me. I don't know what to think."

"Mom, give it time. Neither one of you are going anywhere." Embry smirked. "You could always call Delilah. She would have some good advice for you."

Willow grinned. Her daughter didn't necessarily dislike Delilah, it had more to do with the lack of music being played and all the talking. Secretly, Willow thought Embry hung on every piece of advice the radio personality gave regarding the subject of love. "I think I'll leave that to you. Next time you need relationship advice, I'll look up her number for you. Besides, I don't need relationship advice. I simply don't have one." She squared her shoulders then said, "I don't want to talk about it anymore. I'm fine, really." Then she changed the subject. "What I'd really like to do is talk to some of the baseball players that knew Dean. Perhaps they'll know something that his uncle didn't."

"I'm meeting Marshall for lunch tomorrow, do you want to join us?"

Willow questioned her daughter. "Why would I want to intrude on your lunch, not that I don't want to meet this young man you're dating?"

"Mom, I told you he played baseball."

"You did? When?"

Embry sighed. "Mom, I think you're going a little senile. I told you a couple of weeks ago I was dating a baseball player. He's a nice guy, you'll like him. Why don't you come downtown tomorrow for lunch?"

"Okay, I can do that. Where?"

"There's a little café right on Robinson. We'll meet you there." Embry promised to text the address to her mother.

Willow kissed Embry's cheek before she left and assured her she would be fine unloading without her. Embry had a couple of hours until she had to be at work and she still needed to shower and change, leaving little time for helping to unload. Murder often interrupted normal schedules.

Steve helped Willow unload everything from her truck, wisely discerning she was upset about something therefore keeping his mouth tightly shut. It was good thinking on his part. For the life of him he had no idea what, but he did have a mother and a sister so he knew he didn't have to understand, just go with it and be as sympathetic as possible. When she was good and ready, she would share. He'd learned something about women in his 40 odd years of living.

## This Little Piggy Wound Up Dead

Finally, everything was put in its proper spot and cleaned. He said, "I signed you up for a concealed-carry class at the range. They have several time slots available, just give them a call and let them know which one works best for you."

"Oh, okay. Thanks."

He shifted from one foot to the other. "Do you want to go to the gun show this coming weekend?"

She nodded. "Yeah, I'd like that."

"Great. Maybe we can get dinner afterward."

"Okay." She walked him to his truck. He looked as though he wanted to say something then changed his mind and opened the driver's side door. "I'll give you a call tomorrow after I hear about the autopsy report."

"Oh, yeah, that would be good. Thanks."

He waved and backed out of her driveway.

Willow gathered Clover who had been running around like a mad woman on steroids. Janie had taken good care of her baby while she had been gone. It was already after five and her stomach was rumbling. She hadn't eaten since earlier that morning when she'd made eggs for her little band of barbecuers. She looked through her fridge. Nothing. Cupboard. Again, nothing. She went for the freezer and came out with a pint of rocky road. "This'll do."

She settled on the couch and put in her favorite movie, A Good Year. "Someday," she whispered as she hugged Clover's neck.

# Chapter 6

Willow had to park several blocks away from the downtown Oklahoma City café she'd agreed to meet Marshall and Embry for lunch. She took one look at her heavy purse and tucked it under the front seat of her Jeep. She wasn't carrying that thing through the city streets when she had to walk as far as she did. She put her credit card and her phone in her back pocket and her keys in her front pocket. She groaned as she looked at her McDonald's coffee cup. The night before had been a late one. She'd spent most of it whining to her dog about how unfair life was. At least Clover was a good listener. She also liked the taste of tears, which proved very beneficial. By the time she awoke, the sun was nearly straight above the house, which meant if she didn't get a move on, she was going to be late for lunch. Not making a good impression on Embry's new boyfriend was not an option. Therefore, instead of a leisurely cup of coffee with the paper, she found herself going through the drive-up for her daily dose of caffeine.

# Lilly York

Deciding she needed the rest of her coffee to be anywhere near pleasant at lunch, she removed the cracked plastic lid from the paper cup and proceeded to walk through the city streets, wind and all, sipping her hot coffee and enjoying the city. She was over the night before and feeling sorry for herself. Today was a new day. Coffee helped.

She found the café with no problem and drained the last of her coffee. She looked around for a garbage can to no avail. Her phone beeped. It was Embry. She would be a few minutes late.

Willow leaned against the brick building and watched for her daughter. The café was on a corner so she would look one direction, then the other. The wind was frantic but the sun felt good. For once, the temperature was decent and not threatening to turn her into molten lava. And she was enjoying watching the people as they passed.

Willow had been standing next to the building for nearly five minutes when she looked into her cup and saw a dollar bill. She raised her eyebrows and looked around. "Where did that come from?" She asked out loud, although no one seemed to be paying attention. She shrugged her shoulders and kept watch for Embry. A few minutes later, someone put a five dollar bill in her cup. This time, she caught the person. She raised her hand and started to say something when the stranger cut her off.

"Be sure to use this on lunch. No alcohol, you hear?" He walked away before she could say a word.

Willow was dumbfounded. Why in the world would people be putting money in her cup? She was collecting a fair bit of cash. Lunch was most definitely on her today. She grinned, mentally counting her loot.

An older gentleman who was in desperate need of a shower confronted her. "I don't know what you think you're doing little girl, but this here is my corner."

Willow couldn't help herself. "Really? What is your name?"

"Ned."

"Well, Ned. I don't see your name anywhere. Is this Ned Street? Ned Boulevard perhaps?" She nodded once. "That's what I thought. I can stand here if I like."

He began to protest but a very good looking young man joined the conversation. "Ned, why don't you stand down a little bit today and let the lady have the corner. She could probably use the cash, don't you think?"

Ned seemed to be looking her over. "Yeah, I guess she looks like she could use it. She ain't even got a coat."

The man tucked some cash into Ned's pocket. "There you go. That ought to help." He then turned to Willow. "And this is for you. Make sure you get yourself a good coat before the weather turns colder." He put some cash in her cup. Quite a bit by the look of it. He then went into the restaurant.

A few minutes later, Embry turned the corner. She stopped in her tracks. "Mom, what are you doing?"

"I was waiting for you. Now, we can go in and have lunch." She took Embry's arm. "Is your young man here yet?"

"He was running late too, so I'm not sure. We can go in and wait for him." She looked at Willow's coffee cup and shook her head. "Yeah, I think that's a great idea. If we don't, you're going to get fined for begging without a permit." Embry held the door open for her mother and spotted Marshall sitting in a back corner booth. "Come on, Mom. He's here."

They approached the table and Marshall stood up to greet them, a questioning look plastered across his face. "Embry, this is really nice of you."

## This Little Piggy Wound Up Dead

"What do you mean?"

He nodded toward Willow. "Buying lunch for this homeless lady. I knew you were kind hearted, but I had no idea…"

Embry interrupted. "Marshall, this is my mother."

"Your mother's homeless?" Marshall was shocked.

"No, no" Embry turned to her mother. "Mom, the least you could have done was brush your hair. I mean, really. A little make up won't kill you, ya know?"

"I did brush my hair, thank you very much. I'm not sure if you noticed how windy it is outside. And I had to walk for blocks just to get to the place." Willow picked up the napkin dispenser and attempted to view her appearance. She smoothed down the flyaway hair. "It's not that bad."

Marshall's mouth was open but sound wasn't coming out.

"Yeah, Mom. It's that bad. You look like you live on the street. And why were you standing on the corner anyway? Why didn't you just come in and sit down?"

"I was people watching." She pointed toward a woman leaving the restaurant and Embry pushed her hand down toward the table. "Did you see that woman?" She didn't wait for either of

[40]

them to answer. "Did you see those stockings she was wearing? Unless you're working a street corner, who would wear those to work?"

Embry watched the woman walk away. She was wearing a very short skirt and cut out stockings. "Mom, I'd be careful if I were you. You were the one working a street corner today. Besides, that woman is a prostitute. Some guy brings her to the hotel and they dine at the restaurant several times a month."

Willow's jaw dropped. "You're kidding me?"

Embry shook her head and said to Marshall—who was still speechless—"this is why I rarely take her out. She cannot be let loose in public. You never know what she's going to do or say."

Willow grinned and turned her cup upside down. "Look at all this money. Sheesh…these homeless people make a lot of cash. Lunch is on me today." She looked up and smiled. "Oh, and on Marshall."

It was Embry's turn to be shocked as she looked from her mother to her boyfriend. "You gave her money?"

He just nodded.

Willow stood up. "I need to use the facilities. I drank a lot of coffee." She held the

## This Little Piggy Wound Up Dead

empty paper cup up for them to see then turned and stopped in her tracks. Sitting across the restaurant with yet another guy was Bridget. She took Embry's hand and pulled her to her feet. "Look at who is here."

Marshall, not wanting to be left out, also stood up and looked. "Oh, that's Bridget. She has a thing for the baseball team. The entire baseball team, if you know what I mean."

Embry turned toward Marshall. "Even you?"

He stuttered. "Well, she tried. But, that's not how my mama raised me. She would tan my hide if I ever entered a relationship…like that."

Bridget chose that moment to turn her head. When her eyes rested on Willow, she stopped talking, her eyes widened, and her face turned white. She stood up quickly, made an excuse, and abruptly left the restaurant.

"I wonder what she has to hide." Willow said to no one in particular.

# Chapter 7

Willow sat back down across from Marshall and Embry and smiled. "I feel so much better."

Embry gave her a dirty look. "Bridget sure took off in a hurry. I guess she didn't expect to see us here."

Willow agreed, still wondering why the girl would leave so abruptly if she had nothing to hide.

All three ate their lunch. Willow really liked Marshall. He was kind, even when he thought she was a homeless person.

Embry ordered three coffees and a large slice of chocolate cake to share.

Willow added cream then took a sip. "Mmm, this tastes good. McDonald's coffee really isn't bad though." She got down to business. "Marshall, tell me what you know about Dean Babcock."

Marshall nodded. "Yes, Ma'am."

"Marshall, do you know how old that makes me feel?"

He shook his head.

"Old. As in, call me Willow."

"My mama would…"

She finished his sentence for him. "…skin your hide, yes, I know. We won't tell her."

He looked unsure about Willow's willingness to pull a fast one on his mama. Still yet, he continued. "Dean had real talent. Most of us have to enhance our natural talent with a lot of practice, me included. It seemed as if Dean picked up a bat, ball, or mitt and was an instant success. He didn't have a bad position. He hit just about anything in the zone, he had a great eye, just an all-around natural. You know he was first with the major league, right? He signed the senior year of college. He messed it up and got demoted. Down to the minors to see if he would straighten himself out. He was that good. Seriously."

"Do you know what he did?" Willow took a bite of the luscious cake sitting before her.

"All I know is it almost seemed he was trying to self-destruct. He went out of his way to make sure he didn't succeed."

Willow shook her head. "That is so odd. Who does that?"

Both Embry and Marshall shrugged.

Willow showed Marshall a picture of his face, with the damage done. "Do you have any idea what could have made these marks on his face?"

It was obvious he knew what caused the distinct markings. "I would have to say cleats. But, who would do such a thing?"

"Is there anyone on the team who was mad enough at him to cause this much damage?"

"No, I can't think of anyone. You could always come by the club and ask around. But, he hasn't played with us for months. He's been sitting the bench for so long it's almost like he wasn't on the team. Half the time he didn't show for games, let alone practice. Coach didn't want to cut him permanently in case he got his act together. He was seriously good. Not somebody you wanted to go to another team."

Willow was true to her word and paid the bill. Marshall tried to strong arm her but she insisted. "It's the least I can do." She chuckled.

The three of them left the restaurant and passed Ned as they walked. Willow tucked the cash she collected in his pocket. "Ned, you can have your corner back. I'm getting out of the business."

Willow said her goodbyes and thanked Marshall for the information. She made plans to stop by the club when they came back for a home game later in the week. She had one more errand to run before she headed for home. She looked in

## This Little Piggy Wound Up Dead

her purse to make sure her Taser was handy. Just in case.

As Willow drove, the houses became more and more run down. This was not part of the city she was familiar with, of course, that could be said for most of the city. She finally pulled up in front of a dilapidated structure with kids hanging out playing basketball. Most of them ignored her. A few gave her a curios glance then went on with their game.

The door was open and more kids were streaming around inside the building. Some with cold cans of coke, others munching on hot dogs and popcorn. She looked around, looking for the person in charge.

One little girl with big brown eyes pointed her toward the refreshment counter. Two adults were working handing out food to some of the kids.

Willow watched the comings and goings as children of all ages wandered around. Grade school children were playing with board games and coloring pictures while middle school age kids were playing ping pong and foosball. All a sudden two boys ran into and through the center, one of them passing by her and shoving a blue spray-paint can into her hands. The boy never even slowed down. He did it all in one smooth move. She just watched his retreating backside until they both came to a redwood kind of tree stump of a man. Both boys skidded to a stop.

The entire room went silent for about two seconds then life continued, as if this was a normal occurrence. The man took both boys by the shoulder, motioned with a nod to Willow to follow, and then led them into an office of some sort.

Willow stiffened. She felt as though she had been summoned to the principal's office. Memories of her youth raced through her mind—memories she would rather have forgotten about.

She handed over the can of blue paint and stood at attention. The two boys were standing next to her. For the life of her, she had no idea how she came to be standing in the "what in the world were you thinking" line-up.

A tall thin man entered the room then stopped before her. "Who are you?" She stuck her hand out. "I'm Willow Crier. I'm here to see Mr. Crank."

He took her hand in his and said, "I'm Phillip…" He let go of her hand then held it up to see the blue paint she had just transferred to his hand. "...Crank."

"Oh, Mr. Crank, I'm so sorry." She looked down at her own blue hand and shook her head. "I didn't realize...with everything..." She looked around for help but the two giant body guards were trying to stifle their grins. She wouldn't be able to count on them for support. "It's his fault." She pointed to the boy in the red baseball cap with the letters OU on the front.

"Ms. Crier, are you telling me that boy spray-painted your hand?"

The boy in question, well, teen really, was busy looking at his tennis shoes.

"No, of course, not. I wouldn't let him do that. He just handed me the can when he ran in the building. I had no idea paint was leaking."

At this new information the man holding the can quickly looked down and saw his hand was blue too. He put the can on the table on a paper towel then tried wiping his hand off.

Phillip stepped before the teenagers. "Hold up your hands."

Both boys did as they were told and both sets of hands were covered in various colors of paint.

"What have I told you about defacing property? There are better ways to express yourself than painting on someone else's things."

Willow wanted to leave. She wanted to turn around and pretend she never heard of a troubled boys' baseball team, or Mr. Crank, or Dean Babcock. In fact, she would give just about anything to be back at her ice cream shop dipping out cones and making shakes. A familiar voice caught her attention. Without thinking, she raised her hand to smooth her hair. She turned toward the door.

"Willow, what are you doing here?"

Steve tried not to laugh. She had blue paint in her hair, on her nose, and a swipe running down the side of her cheek.

He turned to Mr. Crank and extended his hand. "Phillip, good to see you."

Mr. Crank held up his hand. "Better not. Unless you want to look like the rest of us, that is."

Steve smiled then took a handkerchief from his pocket and wiped the paint from Willow's nose and cheek. "Here, wipe your hands."

Willow forgot about everything else when his dimple appeared. This man was starting to hold a special place in her heart. She had to be careful. She didn't want a broken heart. She wasn't a young woman like Embry who would probably fall in and out of love a dozen times before she found the man she wanted to settle down with, at least Willow hoped that was the case. She was in her forties and life had a way of slipping right by you if you let it.

She broke eye contact with him and concentrated on her paint soaked hands.

Steve turned to Phillip. "Hey, man. I need to talk to you."

Phillip instructed his two helpers to take the boys to the washroom so they could clean up. "I'll meet you back in here in 15 minutes." He left the conference room and motioned for Steve to follow, who motioned for Willow to follow.

Phillip noticed. "I take it you know this woman?"

"Yeah, and I'm guessing she's here for the same reason I am. The police are looking for members of Dean Babcock's baseball team. You need to get them to come in on their own. It'll be better for them."

Phillip nodded. "So this is about Dean's murder. I figured the police would show up eventually."

"I'm not here in my official role. I'm here as a friend."

Phillip looked sincerely thankful. "Thanks. I appreciate that." He turned to Willow. "Did you come to warn me too?"

"Well, no, not exactly. I wanted to talk with the team."

Both Phillip's and Steve's eyes widened.

"What's wrong with that?"

Steve raised his eyebrows. "The boys who make up this team aren't exactly "sit down for a cup of coffee" kind of guys. They've had a hard life thus far and if given an opportunity, well, let's just say I wouldn't put too much past them."

"So you think they're capable of committing murder?" Willow looked doubtful.

Phillip commented. "Given the right set of circumstances, yes."

It was Willow's turn to look surprised. "But, they're just kids."

"They're kids who have had to grow up faster than most grown adults." As Phillip finished his sentence, there was a loud commotion in the main area of the center. He opened the door to see the police arresting the kid with the red hat.

"Hey, what's going on?" Phillip approached the police officers.

Steve laid his hand on Phillip's arm. "Let me." He flashed his badge and was able to find out what was happening. Then returned to Phillip and Willow.

"Apparently, they recovered the murder weapon. The puncture holes on Dean's face and torso were from cleats. Specifically cleats from the team he was mentoring. That was enough for a search warrant. And they found cleats with blood on them and a bloody knife in Chester's room at his grandmother's house. Chester is being arrested for murder."

# Chapter 8

Willow watched as the broken young man was led outside to a waiting patrol car. "Steve, are you sure they have the right guy?"

He shook his head. "The evidence is pointing that way. If it's not him, he'll be cleared."

Chester's head was downcast as he was guided into the back seat.

Willow's heart was breaking. "Steve, Dean's best friend, Brian, plays golf. Golf shoes have cleats. He also played baseball with Dean on the minor league team."

Steve turned to her. "You're forgetting one thing. The players had blood on their shoes. The same type of blood as Dean's. We can go talk to him, but the kids obviously had a hand in Dean's death. Their shoes put them in the midst of the crime scene. The knife was hidden in Chester's dresser drawer. The team was mad at Dean for not taking their team seriously. Which gives them motive. The only thing we're missing is a confession." He waited for her reaction. "Do you still want to go talk to Brian?"

## This Little Piggy Wound Up Dead

She nodded. "I want to talk to Chester too." She followed along after him. "It just seems too easy. Something isn't right."

"Are you thinking someone planted that knife?"

Willow shook her head. "No, I think he put it there. What I want to know is, why?"

Steve led Willow back out to the parking lot. "Let's go talk to Brian. It certainly won't hurt to see what he has to say. If anything, he might be able to tell us more about Dean."

Willow stuck close behind Steve as he led the way to Brian's house. He had a place in the country. The gates keeping unwanted visitors out indicated the place was very nice. Very nice indeed.

Steve pressed the intercom and was told Brian was not home and not expected until very late and asked if they would return the next morning. Preferably late morning.

After agreeing, he hopped out of his truck and approached Willow's driver side door. "Well, looks like tomorrow will be the soonest we can see him. What now?"

Willow's stomach rumbled and she had an idea. "Are you hungry?"

He smirked.

She rolled her eyes. "Silly me. When aren't you hungry? Let's go to Chilis. The one by the airport. Dean worked there. Maybe someone will know something."

Steve agreed. He would accompany her and hopefully, along the way, she would realize the case was done, over, finished. In the meantime, he would pacify her.

Chilis was nearly empty of all customers. Willow was good with that. She would have more time to question the staff.

Willow and Steve took a seat in a booth, opposite one another and perused the menu. She looked at him over the top.

"By the way, how do you know Phillip Crank?"

"We go to church together. Sometimes I help out at the center."

"Then you knew Dean?"

"No, he didn't come to the center. Phillip handled the community outreach program in conjunction with the judge. This was his way to help keep kids off the street. He gave up a lucrative career in law to run the center. It's his life. He handpicked the boys who were on the team. He feels he has let everyone down. Dean. The city. The system. The judge. Himself. And especially the boys."

## This Little Piggy Wound Up Dead

The waitress interrupted and took their order. He continued. "I only volunteer one Saturday a month. It's all I have time for."

She nodded. "Seems like a good group of people."

He smiled. "They are. So is Philip. He beat the streets. Now he wants to help as many kids as he can do the same."

The waitress returned with their ice teas and cups of enchilada soup.

Willow took a bite. "This is good. I sure do miss their broccoli cheese soup though. I loved that stuff."

It wasn't long before sizzling platters of fajitas were sitting before them.

Willow filled a flour tortilla. "I'm still hungry from yesterday." She devoured her food in record time then leaned back and allowed the waitress to take her dishes. "I'm sorry about your co-worker, Dean Babcock."

"Yeah, we were all shocked. I mean, I know he was into some bad stuff, but you never think it's going to happen to someone you know."

"Did you know him well?"

"No, not really. He was a good worker. A little dark at times, but he pulled his own." The waitress turned to leave then added. "Mindy went to school with him. You should talk to her. She has some stories to tell."

"Is she here?"

"Yeah, I'll have her stop by."

A petite blond girl stopped by a few minutes later. "Clare said you knew Dean. How did you know him?"

Willow answered, "From the barbecue competition. His uncle, Preston, too."

She nodded. "It's real sad, what happened. Everybody in our home town is grievin'. I've known him all my life. Hit me like a ton of bricks."

"Do you know of anyone who would want to kill him?"

Mindy seemed sincere when she said, "No, not a soul. I know he was considered a bad boy every now and again. But, everybody understands that was on account of his sister."

Steve raised his eyebrows. "What happened with his sister?"

"Oh, I best not be telling that story. Mama says gossipin' is of the devil and it's not polite to talk bad about the dead. You best talk to his mama if you want that story. Sides, no one knows what really happened, only that Dean blamed himself. There's all kinds of rumors floatin' around." She lowered her voice to a whisper. "But if you ask me, that girl Bridget had something to do with it. I think that's common knowledge so it won't hurt to go ahead and say it." The hostess sat a table in her section so she told them goodbye and went back to her job.

Willow sat up a little straighter in her seat and whispered, "So, what happened to his sister?"

Steve leaned forward. "Why are we whispering?"

"I don't know. Cause she was?"

He looked around the nearly empty restaurant. "Who are we afraid is going to overhear? There's no one here."

Willow spoke at a normal volume. "Fine. I'll ask again. What happened to his sister? And what in the world did Bridget have to do with it?" She let out a slow breath. "I guess we need to talk to Dean's mama."

Steve agreed. "I guess so." He sighed.

"Steve, there's more to this, I know there is. Chester may have had the knife. And he definitely had a part of stomping on Dean's face and body, but something else is going on." She paused, not sure if she should ask for yet another favor, then again, what the heck. "Do you think you could get me in to see Chester? I just want to talk to him. Hear his story." Seeing his hesitancy, she added, "And maybe after talking to him I'll know he did it. Then we can forget about murder and go on with our lives."

"You promise?"

She held out her pinky. "Pinky swear."

"Huh?"

"Oh, never mind. Yes, I promise."

Mindy may have been tight lipped about Dean's past but every other employee had plenty to say. All through dessert, they heard it all, including Dean smoked dope behind the building during shift hours, he was dealing, he owed everyone money, he stole a customer's car, he broke into people's houses, he was stealing from Chilis, and not just the chips and salsa—said with a wink—he was blackmailing the managers, he was cross dressing, he had a sex change scheduled. If it were possible, Steve and Willow heard it. They were more confused by the time they left the restaurant than they were before they entered. They left the restaurant together and Steve walked her to her Jeep before heading to his truck which was parked in the rear parking lot.

Willow started her vehicle then checked her voicemail and text messages. Mostly Embry. She heard a horn honk behind her. All the front row parking spots were taken and apparently the dude in the truck wanted her space. She ignored him.

## This Little Piggy Wound Up Dead

He honked again. "This guy is getting on my nerves." She murmured.

He laid on the horn and held it there.

"That does it." She turned off her truck, got out, and leaned up against the hood. "Now you've done it. I'm not leaving. I'm gonna stay here all night!"

The guy in the four wheel drive floored it and ended up hitting the light pole in the parking lot. Willow willingly dialed the police for him. "Idiot."

He exited his truck and was cursing all over the place as the police pulled up. Thankfully, they were close by. She pulled up alongside the accident and rolled down her window. "Hey, Mister, I just wanted you to know you can have the parking spot now. I'm done with it." She rolled up her window and pulled away. In her rearview mirror she saw him yelling and waving his hands in her direction.

# Chapter 9

Willow opened the door to The Willow Tree Ice cream Shoppe at 10 the next morning to the smell of freshly baked cinnamon rolls and strong coffee. She began doubting the wisdom in opening a coffee shop in conjunction with the ice cream shop. Even though her bottom line had vastly improved, her age lines also increased. Not good any way you look at it. She was getting less and less sleep. Between murders and working earlier, sometimes her mind just wouldn't shut off. Last night was one of those nights. Every day she was thankful for Janie, who came in for the early morning shift.

Molly, who owned the diner down the street, was standing on the other side of the counter. "Well, look who the cat drug in."

"I guess I do feel like a dead mouse. Do I look like one too?"

Molly laughed. "Oh, phooey. You don't look nothin' like. Just tired is all."

Willow first met Molly when she participated in the town's chili cook-off. She now considered Molly a friend. "What brings you in? Did your coffee machine break?"

"Oh no, nothing like that. Sometimes a girl just wants somethin' different."

Janie, Willow's best friend and sometimes partner in crime, interjected. "If you came in earlier of a morning you'd see Molly comes in almost every day for a cup of our coffee. Sometimes a muffin too."

"This is true. I have to come between the breakfast rush and the lunch rush. This is my change of scenery. I get to breathe here and not have to wait on anyone."

Janie motioned to a table. "It's slow at the moment. Why don't you two sit down and catch up. I'll bring you some coffee and muffins. I made our popular bran muffins this morning as well as lemon poppy seed.

Willow felt guilty. Between the BBQ contest and the murder, she hadn't been doing any of the prep work for the baking.

Janie knew her friend well. "Hey, this is why I get paid the big bucks. You hired me to do this job, remember? I love it. If it was too much, I'd let you know." She pulled out three mugs. "Besides, I'm sitting down for a few minutes too."

Willow carried a tray of muffins and a crock of butter to a three seat table. Janie was close behind with a carafe of coffee, cream, and sugar.

Both Janie and Molly wanted to hear everything about the weekend. While they ate, Willow told them about Dean Babcock. Molly looked alarmed. "I haven't watched the news all weekend. I can't believe I haven't heard about this." Her eyes glassed over.

Willow grasped Molly's arm. "Molly, did you know Dean?"

She nodded. "His mama reached out to our church when her little girl died a few years back. I spent a lot of time praying with her, just being there for her. After a while she stopped going to church. Then she stopped returnin' my phone calls. I figured it was time to let go and give her room to heal. Now she's gone and lost another child." She let the tears flow as Willow and Janie looked on in silence, neither one not knowing exactly how to respond.

Willow waited for Molly to calm down. She hated to ask, but she had to. "Do you know how her daughter died?"

She nodded. "She drowned. It had been stormin' and as soon as the rain stopped, she went outside to explore. Well, I'm not sure if you've experienced one of our flash floods yet, but things can get mighty dangerous mighty quick. And sure enough, she got too close to the creek and got swept away. Everybody was grievin' something awful. Specially her mama and her brother, Dean. Now his mama is going to be buryin' another child. It's just not fair."

"How old was she when she died?"

"She was eight. There were a good number of years between the little girl and her older brother. Their mama never did say who her daddy was. It was all hush hush like. Same with the drownin'. We all thought there must be more to the story cause nothin' was ever said about it later. You know how people talk. Well, there was nothin' to talk about. Nothin' at all."

Willow felt bad to be the bearer of bad news. She had wanted to visit with her friend, not cause her an emotional break down. She sighed. All the more reason to find out who killed Dean and give his mama some closure. It would be hard enough to go forward without being in the dark about who hurt him.

Summer afternoons at the shop were slow so Willow spent the rest of the afternoon baking. She made lemon bars, layered brownies, and cheesecake. Afterward, she felt better, as though she contributed something to her own business.

Janie wouldn't have quite so much to do when she came in the morning.

She was cleaning off tables when Steve swung by the shop a few minutes before she closed. "Hey, what brings you in?"

He took off his hat and held it in his hands. "A couple of things, really. First, are we still on for Saturday afternoon? The gun show?"

"Oh, yeah. I completely forgot. Yes, we're still on. What time?"

"I know your penchant for early mornings, so how does one sound?"

"You know me well. One is perfect. Did you make it back to Brian's?" She had already apologized for not being able to go with him.

"Yes, and once again, he wasn't home," Steve seemed a little nervous.

"Was there something else?"

"Well, um, yeah, there is. You know the center?"

She clarified. "You mean the one we were just at?"

"Yeah, that one. Well, they are having a fundraiser Saturday night."

"I'm glad to hear that. It seems they're really making a difference. I hope they do well with it."

"It's a dinner and dance."

## This Little Piggy Wound Up Dead

She kind of guessed where he was going with this conversation, but she wasn't going to make it easy for him. "That sounds nice."

"Would you like to go?"

"Well, I wasn't invited."

"I'm inviting you now. Would you like to go with me?"

She smiled, relieving his frustration. "Yes, I would be honored to go with you."

He sighed. "Good, I'm glad. It's going to be a formal event, you know, multiple knives and forks—me looking confused as can be, but it should be fun. We'll be sharing a table with my sister and her husband and two other couples from the center."

She asked, "Should we go to the gun show another time? We won't be cutting it too close, will we?"

"You don't think you could manage to get up a little earlier on Saturday, do you? We'd have plenty of time if we went to the gun show in the morning."

"Fine. Fine. I'll get up early. But only because of the kids."

"All right, I'll pick you up at 10." He turned to leave then stopped. "I almost forgot. Dean's funeral is tomorrow. Do you want to go? And I have permission for us to speak with Chester. "He grimaced. "I hate to say it, but we have a 9 o'clock appointment at the jail. I took what they were offering. We can leave straight from the jail and make it in time for the funeral."

"I'll be ready. Bring coffee."

He nodded. "I can't imagine a morning with you without coffee."

She threw her wash cloth at him and he easily stepped aside then left with a smile.

# Chapter 10

Willow let Clover out then brushed her teeth. She glanced at the time then muttered to herself. "Steve will be here in less than 10 minutes. Ugh. I need a few more alarm clocks to set around the room." She was thankful she took a shower the night before. She sure wouldn't have time to take one this morning." She donned her favorite pair of black slip on pants and a maroon short sleeve shirt then circled in front of the mirror. "It will do."

She brushed her hair and noticed the grey skunk stripe just beginning to appear. She tucked the front portion up in a barrette at the top of her head, hoping that would hide the very obvious grey growing out. She would have to dye it before Saturday. She wasn't getting all dressed up just to have her hair look like it belonged on an animal of the night.

A knock on the door, accompanied by barking, let her know Steve had arrived. "I'm almost ready." She said after opening the door. A few minutes later she was back. Her diamond studs and lip gloss finished her funeral attire.

He kissed her cheek. "You look beautiful."

"Thank you." She stepped back. "You don't look so bad yourself." His natural good looks were magnified in his fitted black suit. She wondered if he would wear the same suit on Saturday night. She wouldn't mind walking in on his arm, that was for sure.

It was hard to get her mind off of the good looking man next to her and on the unfortunate young man sitting across from her.

Chester had that defeated look to him. Like he was without hope. A condemned man. Already judged and convicted.

Willow had to drag his story out of him. "Chester, if you don't tell me the whole truth, right now, you will go to prison for the rest of your life. You do know Oklahoma has the death penalty, right?"

His eyes widened. Willow was pretty certain he hadn't considered that fact. He was probably issued a state appointed attorney who was probably over-worked and stretched for time and

## This Little Piggy Wound Up Dead

probably didn't really explain what could happen if Chester was convicted.

Chester shook his head. "I didn't do it."

"How did you get the knife?"

He bit his lip. "I was there with the guys. We wanted to teach Dean a lesson, let him know how much he let us down. We were supposed to have a game and our coach never showed up. He did that sometimes. Like we wasn't important enough, or somethin'. We had to forfeit the game. We worked hard. We coulda' beat em'. So, we called him and told him we needed to talk to him. When he showed up, we taught him a lesson. We each stomped on him to give him a reminder of who he was lettin' down. He was alive when we left him. He was hurtin'. I ain't sayin' he wasn't. But he was alive."

Willow listened intently to Chester's story then said, "That doesn't tell me how you got the knife."

"Well, I was feelin' bad. Dean wasn't such a bad sort. He had his problems. Same as us. So, I went back to check on him. Make sure he was still breathin'. Only thing was—he wasn't there. I just thought he went back to camp. I was leaving when something shinin' in the moonlight caught my eye. I used my phone's flashlight and found that knife. It was covered in blood. I thought one of the guys came back and finished him off. I had to get out of there in case they came back and found me. If they thought I'd gone soft, well, it might be the end of me too." He looked remorseful. "I took the knife. I know I shouldn't have. I sure wish I hadn't."

Willow turned to Steve. "Can we see the knife?"

He was unsure. "I'm sure I can get us access to the pictures of the knife. Would that help?"

She nodded. "Yeah. I'd like to see it."

Steve added. "One thing in your favor, Chester, is whoever stabbed Dean knew exactly where to stab him to cause the most damage. Of course the police are saying you got lucky."

"Man, I didn't stab him. I just went back to check on him. I don't even know where he went."

A detective friend of Steve's brought out some pictures of the murder weapon. Willow was surprised at how small it was and how, well, feminine. She looked closely at the marbled handle. Just big enough for a lady's hand. She would expect a gang member street thug to carry a much larger weapon. "Surely they don't think this little knife is Chester's. I can't imagine he'd be caught dead with that weapon."

Steve interrupted. "Except he was."

She had to give him that. "True. We have to get a move on if we're going to make any part of the funeral."

"You still want to go?"

"Of course, why wouldn't I?"

"Well, I thought we had a deal. You'd let this go if you were able to talk with Chester."

"I said I'd let it go if after talking with him I was convinced he did it. Which, I'm all the more convinced he didn't do it."

Steve closed his eyes for a second them opened them. "Come on. Let's get going."

After leaving Chester, they went straight to the cemetery for the interment. Willow stood at an angle where she could see all her primary suspects' faces. They say the murderer usually attends the funeral to see the work of their hands. Willow was counting on it. Bridget was standing a couple of rows behind the family with a few of the minor league baseball players. Preston was sitting with, or so Willow presumed, his sister in the few folding chairs provided. Standing behind Preston was Brian. Willow had looked him up online. She pointed him out to Steve as they stood surveying the crowd. "Seems he has quite the reputation as a ladies' man." Plural being key in that description. Not one to be tied down, he had a different girl on his arm for each function he attended, including this one. The tall, thin blonde was fashionably dressed and looked his equal in regards to public profiles. Willow wondered who she was.

Willow noticed, what looked like two clergy men talking on the sidelines. Sometimes she wished she had a super hearing super power. Steven nodded to Phillip Crank who was on the opposite side of the coffin. They all waited for whoever was doing the service to take his place by the coffin. Willow noticed a few family members were looking a little confused. She tapped Steve. "I wonder what's going on." She whispered as the pastor or priest or whatever he was began the service. He read from the Bible then prayed. He ended with sprinkling holy water on the coffin and said, "Lord, I commit Michael into your care. Willow leaned into Steve. "I didn't think the family was Catholic and who the heck is Michael?" When he was finished, the other man stood up and read a few scripture and prayed. She commented yet again. "This is confusing."

"Shhh…you're supposed to be watching our suspects. Not the pastor."

"Oh, yeah, you're right. You should see the daggers Bridget is shooting Brian's way. I would say she does not like his date. Huh."

### This Little Piggy Wound Up Dead

A veiled lady in front of them turned around and gave Willow a dirty look.

"Oh, sorry." Willow put her finger to her lips, as if Steve was the one being loud.

He rolled his eyes but remained quiet.

Once the service was complete, Steve went to talk with Phillip and Willow went to chat with Preston and his sister. At least she hoped for a moment with them. She stood on the sideline and waited her turn. The second clergyman was talking with Preston first. She couldn't help but overhear.

"Who is the Catholic Priest?"

Preston looked puzzled. "We thought he was with you."

"No, I've never seen him before. He told me before the service you asked him to handle the interment. Then Michael isn't Dean's middle name?"

"No, we have no idea who Michael is. Nor did we ask the priest to the funeral, let alone to speak graveside."

The pastor crossed his arms. "Huh, I wonder who spoke at Michael's funeral then."

Willow placed her index finger in her mouth and bit down to keep from laughing.

Preston shook the pastor's hand and thanked him for being so understanding. "Even so, it was a nice service."

"Yes it was. I'll see you back at the church for refreshments."

Willow wondered if the priest had to go back to his own church and face Michael's family. She sure wouldn't want to be in his shoes.

Preston's eyes lit up when he saw Willow. He took her hands in his. "It's so good of you to come." He turned to his sister. "Janice, this is Willow. Willow, this is my sister, Janice."

She removed her hands from his embrace and shook Janice's hand. "I'm so sorry for your loss."

"Thank you. You were there when Preston found my son, right?"

"Yes, I was there."

Her eyes misted over. Willow was surprised she had any tears left.

Janice looked to her brother. "We better be gettin' on over to the church. People will be there waitin' on us." She turned to Willow. "Will we see you there?"

"Yes, I believe we'll be there." She hoped Steve knew which church the luncheon was at or they just might end up at the Catholic Church with Michael's family.

# Chapter 11

"I didn't plan on going to the church."

"How else are we going to see how everyone reacts to one another? This could be quite telling." Her stomach grumbled. "Besides, I'm hungry. Guaranteed they'll have a pretty good spread. Funerals usually bring out the best cooks."

Steve perked up. "This is true. I hadn't thought of that."

"How is Phillip holding up?"

Steve shook his head. "Not the greatest. He's still wondering what he could have done to prevent the whole mess. Five of his students are being held in lock up. Unless the evidence proves otherwise, Chester is going to be tried as an adult. He's losing sleep with worry." He changed lanes then added. "And he has this fundraiser on top of everything else. He can't reschedule. It's too late. He'll lose the money he's invested and the center will go under."

"Everything's going to work out. Trust me, it will. And the fund raiser is going to be a raging success."

"How do you know?"

"Cause, I just do."

He pulled into the church parking lot and shut the truck off. Both he and Willow remained seated. Willow glanced at Steve's profile. He was staring straight ahead in obvious thought.

She interrupted and asked, "Did anyone find Dean's cell phone?"

"Oh, not that I know of. They had ordered his phone records and were expecting them this afternoon. I'm sure I'll be able to see them when they do."

She nodded, "Good, I'd like to see them too." She turned to him. "Are you ready?"

"Yeah, let's go. Should we split up after we eat and see what we can find?" He looked at his watch. "What do you say we meet back here in an hour?"

"An hour? I think we'll need more like two."

"Fine. Two it is." He opened his truck door. "But first, we eat."

Her stomach spoke for her so she just nodded her head.

People were already seated at long, end-to-end tables with what appeared to be casserole heaven on their plates. Because she generally cooked for one, she rarely made casseroles. On the rare occasion she did, even though she knew she wasn't supposed to, she ended up sharing a little with Clover. The rest she threw away. So, she refrained even though on occasion her sought after chicken enchilada recipe somehow made it into her oven. She was pretty certain Embry could smell that baking from the city as she always showed up as Willow was pulling it out of the oven.

She tried to get a good look at everyone's plate as they walked through the building and to the families' sitting area. Too many tuna casseroles and not even chicken enchiladas. *What is the world coming to?*

Even though Willow had already expressed her condolences, Steve had not. He had yet to meet Janice. Preston, he remembered well. Still, etiquette demand he behave properly and not give into the jealousy that was tugging at his heart. He extended his hand and a smile. "Good to see you again, Preston."

Preston nodded knowing full well Steve was the competition. "This is my sister, Janice."

"Ma'am." He took her slight hand in his own.

Just as Willow opened her mouth to speak, someone from the kitchen yelled out, holding a landline in her hand. "Is Father Jericho here? St.

Luke's is looking all over for him. It seems he never showed up at the cemetery."

Steve looked at Willow. "What are you laughing at?"

"Oh, nothing. I'll tell you later."

He shrugged his shoulders. "You ready to get something to eat? I see Detective Martin is in the food line. Let's join him. Maybe he has some new information."

The three of them took their loaded plates and found a quiet end of a table. Willow did all the talking for the first five minutes. The guys were too busy eating.

"Detective, is there any way I can see the evidence? I still don't believe Chester killed Dean. Yeah, he kicked him with his cleats on and yeah, he took the knife. But he didn't kill him. I'm sure of it."

The detective wiped some barbecue sauce off his chin. "Believe it or not, we really do want to put the right guy behind bars. But, we have to go where the evidence takes us. Fact, Chester's cleats had the victim's blood on them. Fact, a knife with the victim's blood and Chester's finger prints were found in Chester's room at his grandmother's house. We can place him at the scene of the crime. We know he has a motive and we certainly know he has a temper. The only thing we are lacking is a confession."

Willow sucked her breath in. "You're beating it out of him, aren't you?"

Steve and Martin both started laughing. "You watch too many crime shows."

Martin put his hand out to quiet Steve. "No, we aren't beating it out of him. His insistence on being innocent has given us reason to go over the evidence again to see if we are missing anything. We want the murderer behind bars. Not an innocent man." He paused. "If he is innocent, that is." He took a swig of his tea. "And to answer your question, I don't see a reason why you and Steve can't take a look at the evidence. Come back to the station with me and I'll get you set up."

Willow smiled victoriously until she heard raised voices. Turning, she saw Bridget arguing with Brian, Dean's best friend, well, former best friend. And just who she needed to talk to. Bridget was an enigma. She was all over the place, in everyone's business. For a person who seemed as though she had something to hide she was everywhere. Willow was having a tough time sizing her up. Which reminded her to go back to the hospital.

Brian was keeping his voice low, Bridget, on the other hand was raising her voice. Brian was looking around, gauging who was paying attention and who wasn't. Bridget didn't seem to care who was listening. He was obviously concerned someone would over hear what she was saying. Dean was definitely the subject of their conversation. Willow excused herself and wandered closer to where they stood, hoping to hear something of value.

She leaned against the wall just around the corner from the arguing couple, hoping she wasn't too obvious, and listened to the accusations.

"You got too greedy, Brian. You wanted more and look what happened."

"You don't know what you're talking about. You better shut your mouth before someone overhears you."

"Good! Maybe you'll pay for what you've done."

"Done? I haven't done anything."

She heard a bit of a scuffle and then Bridget said, "Don't you ever touch me again. I'm warning you, you ever lay a hand on me again and your nasty little secret will have the world's ear."

Another voice, one Willow recognized joined the discussion. "This is not the time nor the place. We'll discuss this later."

Suddenly the voices halted. Willow edged closer to the bend in the wall just as Bridget stepped around the corner. "You again? You really need to learn to mind your own business." Bridget pushed passed Willow and headed for the door.

Willow turned to see Brian leaning against the wall in a relaxed pose, arms crossed, and a crooked grin plastered against his face.

"I heard you've been looking for me."

"Looks like I've finally found you."

He nodded in the direction Bridget had just left. "I wouldn't pay any mind to anything Bridget has to say. Drama is her drug of choice."

"And yours is avoidance?"

He laughed. "Good one, but no. I've been busy. I haven't avoided anything." He looked her up and down. "Or anyone."

Willow involuntarily shuddered. He was good looking but somehow his looks only served to further his creepiness. "Good to hear. I thought you might have something to hide."

He laughed again. "Don't we all?" He shifted and stood upright. "Well, I'm here now. Ask me anything you want."

Willow felt Steve's presence before she heard his voice. She was glad to have him nearby. She wasn't one to make snap judgements about anyone, but this guy had some bad mojo about him. She took a step backward and bumped Steve's shoulder.

Steve, apparently not getting the same vibe as she did, took a step forward and stretched out his hand. "Steve Grice."

Willow noticed he didn't attach police chief to his name.

Brian met him halfway. "Brian Wilson."

Steve nodded. "I'm sorry for your loss."

Willow watched as Brian's demeanor softened. He became almost human. "Yeah, it's been tough."

"We're trying to figure out what happened. Anything you can help us out with? I know you two were close. I'm sure you want to see his killer brought to justice."

Brian shook his head. "Yeah, I wish I could help but I've got nothin'. Even though he had his share of problems, he didn't deserve what he got."

Steve placed his hands on his hips then asked, "I heard Dean worked for you."

This question caused Brian to make eye contact with Steve. "Not sure where you heard that but you heard wrong. Dean worked for Chilis."

"Oh, I know he worked for Chilis. But someone told me he did some work for you on the side." Steve watched Brian's reaction.

Brian was fidgeting. Obviously nervous. Willow watched as his aloofness dissipated. "A long time ago maybe, but not recently. I'm sure whoever said that was just confused. He was a druggie. I wouldn't have him working for me. Our friendship didn't run that deep."

"That's kind of harsh. Your best friend just died. I was under the impression relationships described as best friends ran pretty deep."

"Yeah, well, things change." He glanced at his watch. "Look, I gotta get out of here. I'm running late. I hope you find whoever it is who did this thing."

Willow and Steve stood side by side and watched Brian walk through the exit. They followed him and noticed a couple of Mexican muscle men talking to him in the parking lot. They used a lot of hand gestures before getting into a large 4x4 truck and following behind Brian's Mercedes.

Steve commented, "I've got a bad feeling about this guy. Not sure if he's responsible for Dean's death, but he sure isn't on the up and up, that much is for sure."

Willow nodded and before she could comment, Preston chose to join them. She glanced at Steve but kept quiet. She had no idea how much Preston overheard and she certainly didn't want to give him anything else to chew on.

"I see you finally met Brian."

Willow was grateful. He may have been stating the obvious but at least he wasn't serenading her. "Yep. It was a bit anticlimactic."

"I can understand that."

Willow wondered if Preston was throwing Brian under the bus to save his own hide. She was still at a loss. Preston had 50,000 reasons for being upset with Dean. Bridget had a few and Brian seemed to have none. At least so far. The one thing she knew for certain was, Chester may be a trouble maker, but he wasn't Dean's killer. She was 100% sure. Well, make that 99%.

Steve and Willow met Detective Martin back at the station and looked over the evidence. Dean's phone records were the first thing that caught Willow's eye. She noticed several numbers with multiple calls. Some lasting mere seconds while others lasted a few minutes or even longer. She noted the numbers so she could do a reverse look up from her computer later. She wanted to know who Dean had been in contact with leading up to and the night of his murder.

Steve was looking at the knife. "You're right. This isn't the type of knife I would expect a gang member to be carrying." The knife, with its mother of pearl inlay, was also carved. It was a beautiful piece. He looked closer. There was script of some sort. He was having a hard time focusing.

## This Little Piggy Wound Up Dead

"Willow, can you read this?" He held the plastic bag up for her to get a closer look.

Detective Martin interjected, "Oh, we had to read it with a magnifying glass. It says Mexico."

Willow replayed the scene outside the church. A couple of Mexican strong men and Brian Wilson arguing. *Exactly what kind of business is Brian in?*

# Chapter 12

The next morning Willow dropped Clover off at the groomers for her appointment. What she would give for a day at the spa. *Yeah, like that'll happen anytime soon.* Might be a good idea for Christmas for her and Embry. She tucked the idea away in her mental planner. She grimaced as her big toe on her right foot pressed against the inside of her shoe. *Before anyone is touching my foot I'll have to have this ingrown toenail taken care of.*

She hated the idea of it, but as soon as life settled down a little, pretty much as soon as this murder was solved, she'd have to make an appointment to have it cut out. Six years before she had the procedure done. It took 15 shots to numb her toe enough so the doctor could cut away the nail. She was not looking forward to a repeat performance. Yet she couldn't put it off. Every time her toe so much as brushed against the bed sheet, she woke up. So much for getting a good night's rest.

Willow took the elevator to the third floor. She glanced around on the lookout for Bridget.

## This Little Piggy Wound Up Dead

She wanted information but she didn't want to cross paths with the unfriendly woman if she didn't have to. She approached the nurses' desk and waited for the woman on the phone to finish up.

"Can I help you?"

"Yeah, I'm looking for Bridget Tully."

The older lady replied. "You and me both." She rubbed the back of her neck. "If you happen to find her tell her she's fired. This is the third time this week she's not showed for her shift. And the second time I've had to cover for her. If she doesn't need this job, there are plenty who would be mighty happy to take her place." She narrowed her eyes. "Who are you, anyway?"

Willow tried to look ornery, "Disgruntled patient. Just wanted to give her a piece of my mind. She assisted with my toe surgery. She had a bad attitude."

The nurse looked confused but didn't question Willow. "She's had a series of formal complaints lately. I thought she was such a good nurse when she first signed on. She cared about her patients and was always on time for work. Lately it's like she is so distracted when she is here, she might as well not be."

Willow's phone began buzzing so she took a few steps backward. "Thanks for the help and if

I come across her, I'll let her know you're looking for her."

The phone rang again so Willow beelined for the elevator. Willow waved goodbye to the staring nurse as the elevator doors began to close. Her phone stopped buzzing before she could answer. Not that she had a signal in the elevator.

She called Steve back once she got situated behind the wheel of her truck. "Hey, what's up?"

"Where are you at?"

She pinched her lips together. He would not be pleased. "I'm at the hospital."

"What happened? Are you okay?"

"I'm fine. Just had an errand to run."

"Wait a minute. You're there checking up on Bridget, aren't you?"

"The little good it did me. She didn't show up for work today. Which happens to be the third day this week she's missed."

"Well, she had a pretty good reason for missing today."

"Oh? What's that?"

"Her body was found downtown in an alley. In a not so great neighborhood."

"Body, meaning no longer alive?"

"Yep."

"I take it she didn't die from natural causes?"

"Broken neck. Someone snapped her neck like she was nothing more than a twig. Had to be someone she knew and it had to be someone who could over power her pretty easily."

Willow sighed. "I didn't like the girl, I mean, I haven't met anyone who actually did like her, but she certainly didn't deserve this. Do you think her murder is related to Dean's?"

Steve was silent on the other end of the line for a few seconds then replied. "I don't know. I think it would be too much of a coincidence to have two people who knew each other intimately be murdered within days of one another and not be connected."

"I'm thinking so too." Another thought cheered her up. "Do you think this gets Chester off the hook?"

"Don't start counting your chickens before they hatch. One step at a time. Just because they're related doesn't mean the same person murdered both of them. We have to figure out what is going on. There is definitely something going on."

Willow ended the call with Steve and immediately dialed the number Marshall gave her. After a quick explanation and a short drive, she found herself surrounded by baseball players in various forms of dress. She was thankful for the opportunity to speak to the team as a whole, but she would have chosen a pizza place or, well, any place other than the locker room. The catcalls kept her from asking any questions. It seemed every guy knew she was uncomfortable and they knew exactly what to say to keep her face flushed a deep red. Marshall stepped in and called for some semblance of order.

"Hey guys. The lady needs to ask us about Dean. Can you show a little respect? And for goodness sake, keep yourselves covered. She's not a reporter looking for a story. She's trying to help solve the murder of one of our own."

Willow was thankful. The ball players cooperated and as long as she kept eye contact with every person she spoke with and never allowed her gaze to drift lower than shoulder height, she was able to keep from turning crimson. She doubted the team had anything to do with Dean's murder but since they had a bbq team at the competition and had a relationship with Dean, well, she had to at least cross them off the list. It turned out the only reason they were even at the competition was one of their sponsors was a local stockyard. They entered to promote their sponsor. And it was good PR for the team.

Marshall walked Willow to her truck. "Sorry about that. The guys aren't all from around here. Not all of them are Southern gentlemen. They

## This Little Piggy Wound Up Dead

didn't mean anything by how they acted. You just gave them the opportunity to act out. During season everyone maintains a strict everything, diet, no partying, practice and drills every day, they don't get much of a chance to just be, well, guys." He kicked up a little dust. "And most of them are pretty young. They're used to making a ruckus."

She smiled. "It's okay. I have to admit I was a bit embarrassed and surprised, but, I lived. I only have a daughter. I've not raised up any young men."

He laughed. "Well, you'll find we're a whole other breed."

She nodded. "I have to agree."

They both laughed then Marshall turned serious. "Did you find out anything today? Anything at all that will help you figure out what happened?"

"No, not really. Dean was arguing with his uncle. That we already knew. He was arguing with Bridget—which we also knew. I guess there was one surprise. Brian didn't have much contact with Dean at the park. Apparently they were at odds with one another. Brian stuck close to their camp. He did have the night shift though, watching the smoker. Same as Dean. I guess it's something we'll have to look into."

He opened her door for her and she climbed in and rolled down her window. "It would appear you have something you'd like to say. Maybe something that has nothing to do with Dean?"

It was Marshall's turn to blush. "Yeah, I just wanted to tell you how much I like your daughter. She really is something."

She studied him. "Yep. I know. She's pretty special." She started the Jeep. "Marshall, don't break her heart. If you aren't looking for the real deal, end it now. Embry is tender hearted and she tends to give a lot more in a relationship than she gets." Willow smiled. "Did you know I'm getting my concealed carry permit? I'm going to get my gun on Saturday."

He touched the brim of his hat. "I did not know that, um, thank you for filling me in though." He smiled back. "Point taken. I'll do my best to tread gently."

"You do that, Marshall."

Willow had one last stop before she had to pick up Clover and head home.

## This Little Piggy Wound Up Dead

She parked in front of the small boutique and braved the front door. Her heart was rapidly beating. She played it cool when Steve asked her to attend the fund raiser, but inside, she was falling apart. She had nothing to wear. She entertained the idea of asking Embry for help then changed her mind. There would be plenty of time to spill her guts after the date was over. For a few days she felt like Cinderella getting ready for the ball and she kept the secret to herself. She even had an appointment to get her nails and hair done. She self-consciously ran her hand through her hair.

She glanced around the shop. She wasn't certain they carried her size. She wasn't exactly petite.

A sales lady approached her. "Hi, can I help you with something?"

"I'm looking for a dress. Uh…"

The well-dressed woman took a step back and eyed Willow. "I'd say a size 12? And I'm guessing this is for something special?"

Willow nodded.

The lady smiled. "Follow me. I have something that will knock him dead." She started toward the back of the shop and stopped in front of a rack of little black dresses. "She pulled a dress off the rack and held it up to Willow. "Why don't you try it on and see what you think." She pointed to the dressing room.

Willow took the silky dress and pulled the curtain closed. She allowed the soft material to glide over her head and down her back. She turned in a circle as the dress swished against her legs. It fell just above the knee. Respectable and perfect for summer. The sleeveless garment reminded her of something Audrey Hepburn would wear. Feminine, demure, and yes, sexy, in a simple unassuming way. She loved it. It was perfect.

She opened the curtain and stood before the full length mirrors.

"I knew it was perfect for you. Just perfect." She motioned for Willow to turn in a circle. "Well, what do you think?"

"I'll take it."

"I thought as much."

Willow quickly changed and handed the dress over to be packaged. The bill surprised her a little. She'd never spent so much for so little material. She didn't care. She never did such things and this time, she was going to go all out. She wanted the evening to be special. In order for that to happen, she had to feel special. This dress did just that. She handed the woman her credit card without hesitation.

# This Little Piggy Wound Up Dead

Willow whistled as she walked back to her Jeep. She couldn't wait to see the look on Steve's face. One way or another, he was going to have to confront his feelings for her. This dress would act as the catalyst to make that happen. She just knew it.

# Chapter 13

Willow used some downtime at the café to look up the numbers from Dean's cell phone records. The first number belonged to Preston. No surprise there. Then there was Brian's and Bridget's numbers. Again, no surprise. What took her by surprise was a long list of numbers he called only once that were a minute or two in length. A reverse lookup did not provide her with any information. She took a chance and dialed the first number on the list.

"Hola."

"Hello. Who is this?"

"No hablo ingles."

Willow heard a click on the other end of the line. She held the phone out and dialed the next number on the list and once again she received the same response. In fact, she received the same response for every number Dean used only once on the same day nearly at the same time. Which happened to be a week prior to his death. "How odd."

"What's odd?"

## This Little Piggy Wound Up Dead

She smiled at Embry. "I didn't hear you come in." She stood and gave her daughter a hug.

Embry looked over her shoulder. "What ya working on?"

"Oh, well, I'm trying to figure out who these numbers belong to. It's Dean's call log." She pointed to a long list of numbers. "There must be at least 15 numbers here and each one says they do not speak English then they hang up. That's all I've got."

Embry poured herself a glass of ice tea and joined her mother. "Well, the key is to find what each of these people have in common. Or perhaps who they have in common."

"Besides Dean, you mean."

"Well, yes. Of course. There must be some reason he was calling these Hispanic families. But why?"

"I saw Brian talking with, what looked like, a group of Hispanic muscle men. I wonder if Brian is the common denominator."

"We could always follow him and see where he leads us."

"You'd go with me?"

"Sure. Why not."

"Are you off Friday?"

"Sure am. Should I come here Thursday night?"

"Enchiladas for dinner?"

"Now you're talking."

The door to the café opened and both ladies spent the rest of the evening making ice cream cones, shakes, and lattes. Willow smiled as she watched Embry interact with their clientele. Someday this would be hers. To see her enjoying herself meant the world to Willow. She knew she was building a legacy to pass down to generations that came after her.

Willow woke before the alarm clock. She couldn't remember the last time that happened. She showered then dressed in a pair of capris and a light summer tank top before leaving for her morning appointment. Janice, Dean's mom, agreed to share their story with her. Of course she hoped it would solve the mystery of who murdered him. Willow sincerely hoped it would.

Willow was surprised to see Janice lived in a really nice gated community. She didn't get the impression from Molly that Janice was well off. At least she didn't have to worry about finances at a time like this. They say money doesn't buy happiness but not having enough sure does cause stress.

She rang the doorbell and was promptly greeted by the woman of the house.

## This Little Piggy Wound Up Dead

"Willow, please come in."

Willow followed Janice into a well-appointed sitting room. She already had refreshments laid out and poured Willow a glass of ice tea.

"Please, help yourself to a Klobasnek. Or maybe two. They're very good." She pointed to a tray of pastry looking puffs. "There are also some mini quiche and some fruit. I wasn't sure what you normally eat for breakfast so I made a variety."

After taking a bite of the delicious sausage filled pastry, Willow said, "Thank you. I sure wasn't expecting this. This is delicious. I thought they were called Kolaches."

"No, although most people do call them that. Kolaches are actually pastry that have a hole in the middle that is filled with sweets. Klobasneks are completely enclosed and you don't get to know the filling until you take a bite. Delicious is what I call them."

"I can see why." She wiped some juice from the corner of her mouth. "Thank you for agreeing to see me."

Janice nodded. "If there's anything I can do to bring my baby's killer to justice, then it's my duty."

"I know this is going to be painful for you. I'm sorry for that. But I have to ask. What happened with your daughter and how was Dean involved?" The grimace that flashed across the woman's face was obvious. She hadn't been expecting the question Willow posed. "I know this brings up memories that you are still healing from. I feel like I need to understand Dean to understand how he came to be in a place where someone would want him gone."

Janice stood up and stared out the glass wall that separated them from the heat of the morning. "He never stopped blaming himself. For what happened, that is." She turned to Willow. "He was home from college. So full of himself. So sure of himself. It was spring break. I had to run to the city and he was supposed to be watching his sister. Instead he was having a make out session with his girlfriend. Bridget Tully. She wouldn't give him the time of day in high school. Once his college team figured out how talented he was, and he became the star of the team, she was attached to him at the hip. Funny how that happens."

She poured herself a drink. Willow dare not look at her watch but it couldn't be much past 10:30.

Janice took a long swallow of the amber liquid then continued. "As soon as she heard he was home, she was at the house like clockwork. What a hussy. She was all over him too." She turned to look at Willow. "You've seen her. She's a trophy girlfriend. At least in the looks department. He thought he'd died and gone to heaven. To think a girl like her would be interested in a guy like him. Well, that day we had record rainfall which caused the creeks and rivers to swell. Flooding is a terrible problem for us in the spring time. The rain had finally subsided and being 8, Mimi's natural curiosity got the better of her. She ventured outside even though I told her firmly to stay inside. She had a tendency to do exactly what she wanted to do.

"No one really knows what happened after that. It could have been anything swirling around in the water that caught her interest. A toy. A dog. We just don't know. The neighbor looked out the window just in time to see her wade into the water a little and reach for something. The next thing he knew she was knocked off her feet and swept downstream. He called 911 and ran outside but there was no sign of her. She was gone. We found her the next day a few miles south. Her clothing got caught on a felled tree and as the waters subsided..." Janice finished her drink and poured another. "You get the idea."

Willow had no words. Nothing that could possibly make a difference to the mother who lost her child. Make that two children.

"Afterward, Dean started punishing himself. He had caught the eye of the scouts for the MLB and had already been offered a place on a pro team. Within the first few months he was let go and sent down to the minors. The team said when he got his act together he would get another chance. Most people chalked up his actions to youthful indiscretions. But we all knew it was because of Mimi. He managed to get on the team here in the city. He got into all kinds of trouble and hung with the wrong kind of people. It was almost as if he was on a mission to get himself killed." She turned a sad gaze to Willow. "I didn't lose Dean Saturday. I lost him the day I lost Mimi."

Willow felt she understood Dean a lot better after talking with his mother. She offered to help clean up but Janice insisted she had daily help, thanks to her brother, Preston.

"No, we've got this. I have a young gal who comes in every day to help me with the house chores. She doesn't speak a lick of English, but Preston speaks Spanish and does a great job of conveying what I need done. She's gotten quite good at domestic help. I don't think I could survive without her." Janice turned toward a closing door. "Ah, here she is now. She's been in the back half of the house catching up on laundry and dusting." She motioned to the pretty young girl she was ready to have the dishes picked up. "Willow, you must take some of this home with you. I'll never eat it all. Not in a million years and then it will go to waste."

Willow followed Janice to the kitchen and looked around while waiting for her leftovers. They would make a great lunch. In fact, she might think about making those Klobasneks for the coffee shop. She was pretty certain they would be a hit."

Like most mothers, Janice had pictures on her refrigerator. One of the pictures was of Dean with his arm around a young darker skinned girl Willow assumed was Mimi. "Is this your little girl?"

Janice came to stand behind Willow. "Yes, that's my Mimi. I miss her so much."

Willow ran her finger across a picture of Preston with a group of young Hispanic men. She looked a little closer. She was certain she'd seen these men before. Then she remembered. These were the same men who were arguing with Brian the day of the funeral. *What in the world is Preston doing with that bunch?*

"I see you've spotted Preston. Those are the guys who work for him on his farm. They're a good group of guys. In fact, Clara is related to one of them. I can't remember which one though."

"Preston has a farm? I thought he'd always wanted to open a food truck."

"Oh, he jokes about it from time to time but it's nothing he takes very seriously. He's really busy with his farm. Besides, he makes excellent money. He's a wonderful brother. I'm so thankful for the help he gives me. I certainly wouldn't be living here if it weren't for him."

Willow left in a bit of confusion. She thought Brian was the one employing the thugs from the funeral. How could she have been so wrong?

# Chapter 14

Embry read off the list of inventory for the stakeout. "Snacks. Cooler for drinks. Drinks. Newspaper."

Willow interrupted. "Newspaper?"

Her daughter looked up from her list. "Yeah, you know. If we have to sit on a park bench and pretend we're reading the newspaper."

Willow scratched her head while Embry continued.

"Dark glasses, hats, binoculars, camera, video recorder, notebook, phone charger, fake mustaches, and a large empty two liter bottle with a funnel…."

"An empty two liter with a funnel?" Willow had a good idea where this was headed.

"Mom, how are you going to make it without a bathroom within ten feet of you?"

"You expect me to pee in that?"

"Well, if you get desperate enough…"

"I hate getting old!"

"Is there anything else you can think of?"

"I think you've got it covered. I couldn't imagine anything else we might need." Willow watched as each item was placed back in the duffle bag, including the two liter bottle. "We better eat something. Not sure if we'll get a chance later. Who knows if Brian stops to eat while he's out."

Embry rubbed her stomach. "I'm still stuffed from last night. I think coffee will suffice."

Willow took out the leftovers she was sent home with and popped them in the microwave. "Suit yourself. I'm going to eat a little something."

The smell got to Embry and she ended up helping Willow finish off the food. Willow let Clover back in. "You realize it's still dark out, right?"

"Mom, we have no idea what time Brian leaves the house. We have to be in position and ready. We don't want to miss him."

"Yeah, yeah. I know. Whose crazy idea was this anyway?"

Embry gave her a dirty look.

They loaded Embry's car just in case Brian knew what Willow's Jeep looked like and started off for the city.

She stopped to top off the tank and for Willow to use the bathroom, one last time, before they stalked their prey.

## This Little Piggy Wound Up Dead

Willow wiped the sweat from her brow. "Should it be this hot this early? This is ridiculous."

"Mom, we can't keep the car running. Someone might notice." As it was, they were cramped in the back seat of Embry's little economy car. Embry looked up the proper way to run a stake out and apparently the front seat was a big no no.

Thankfully they did not have to wait long. When Brian's Mercedes pulled out of the drive, Embry was only a few seconds behind him. Embry did a good job of keeping her distance and remaining obsolete. She pulled into a parking space at a café and watched Brian go in for breakfast.

"Can't we go in? I'm hungry."

"No, we'll completely blow our cover."

Embry grinned "Don't you want to know if he's meeting someone? Besides, he doesn't know me."

Willow relented. "Keep me posted. And don't get noticed."

Embry put a baseball cap on and took the newspaper. "I'll be back in a jiffy." She slammed the door behind her and left Willow to wait it out. Not that Willow was any good at waiting. Not really her strong suit. At all.

Finally, after what seemed an eternity, Embry exited the restaurant with a white Styrofoam container in hand. "I brought you something." She handed Willow the container.

Willow breathed in deeply. "Smells delicious. What is it?"

"Their special. Breakfast burrito."

Willow sunk her teeth in the tasty breakfast sandwich and listened as Embry filled her in.

"I was able to sit at a table near to his. You won't believe who he was having breakfast with."

Willow raised her eyebrows. "Who?"

"Your opera singing crush."

"Preston?"

"Yep. Seems he was already there waiting on Brian. He already had his plate of food and was half finished when the waitress was taking Brian's order."

"Embry, Preston knows you. He's seen you."

"Mom, I have no make-up on. I'm wearing a baseball cap. My hair is in a bun. I'm wearing an OU t-shirt and a pair of jeans. I'm about as invisible as I can get. He didn't even notice I was there. Neither of them did."

"Could you hear their conversation?"

"Some of it. And yes, Dean was brought up a couple of times. I left before he did so I would keep up my cloak of invisibility." She pointed to the door. "So, we need to keep an eye out for him. We don't want to miss him."

"What else did they say?"

"Something about a new shipment coming in tomorrow. Would Brian be able to take care of it since Dean was no longer among the living."

"Huh. Preston's sister did say something about him having a farm. Maybe Brian works for Preston. Although I highly doubt it. I can't see him slinging slop, can you?"

Embry laughed. "No, although that would be something!"

"For some reason I thought Brian owned his own business. He lives well enough. He has to have some serious money coming in from somewhere." Willow watched him exit the restaurant and leave the parking lot. "Let's keep with the original plan. I still think Brian is the key to all this. He knows something."

Embry followed behind, once again remaining close enough to see where he was going and far enough back to blend in with the rest of traffic.

"You're going to lose him. Don't let him get too far ahead."

"Mom, I'm not going to lose him. I know what I'm doing."

Willow looked sideways at her daughter. "You know what you're doing? As in, you've done this before?"

"Yeah. I've done this before. Maybe not for the same reasons, but I've done it."

"Embry. Why in the world were you tracking someone and why don't I know about this?"

"Mom, you don't know everything about me, ya know?" She made a left turn and kept driving. "I was helping a college friend tail her boyfriend. She was pretty sure he was cheating on her and sure enough, we caught him red handed. Well…at least his face was red handed when she knocked on the car window."

"Oh, that's terrible. What a jerk."

"No kidding. That's why I helped her."

"Oh, look!" Brian turned onto a dirt road then through a gated driveway. "How are we going to follow him now?"

"How about we drive around a long block and see if we can see anything?"

"Okay"

"And keep your eyes out for any type of covering…in case we have to hoof it."

"Hoof it…as in walk?"

"Yep." Embry glanced at Willow's feet. "You wore your hiking boots, right?"

"Yeah."

"Well, that's the reason I told you to wear them."

"Oklahoma isn't exactly known for terrain that you can blend in."

"Oh, no worries. We'll be discreet."

They drove around the country block and found the land was one big property with a nice size house right in the middle.

Willow noticed some workers in a field. "Hey, maybe this is Preston's farm."

"That would be my guess."

The dust from Brian's car settled near the house. Embry found a turn in from the opposite side of the block near a patch of trees. It seemed to lead into the same field. "Let's park the car here and see if the workers know anything."

Willow shrugged. "Okay. I guess it's worth a shot." Willow squeezed her thighs together. "Do you think I've got enough cover?"

"Mom. Hurry up. I'll keep watch."

"Okay, I'll lookout for you next."

"Oh, that's okay. I don't have to go."

"No?"
"I went at the café."
"Ugh! Traitor."
"Would you hush and hurry up?"

Willow and Embry approached the workers like it was a normal every day activity. Willow spoke nearly no Spanish and Embry was marginally better.

"Hello, hola." Embry called out as they approached the workers nearest them. They all stopped checking watermelons and stood up, not sure what to think.

It was then Willow had a bright idea. She quietly took out her cell phone and dialed one of the numbers that were on Dean's list. She noticed one of the workers answer his phone, look at it, then hang up. She did this several times while Embry was trying to get information from the immigrant workers. A few of the calls were picked up by men in the field.

"Now I'm getting somewhere."

"Mom, they have no idea whatsoever what I'm saying. And the little Spanish I do know is getting no reaction from them." She looked around at the workers who were all silently staring at the two white women interrupting their work. "Oh, here comes someone. Maybe they can help."

## This Little Piggy Wound Up Dead

Willow looked up just in time to see one of the bulky men Brian was speaking with at the funeral heading straight for them, with a gun no less. Brian was not far behind. "Embry, run!"

Both women ran as fast as they could for the car. Someone was shouting behind them, not that they stopped to listen to what was being said. After leaving dust flying everywhere, Embry was the first to catch her breath. "Mom, what in the world is going on? Why would that guy have a gun?"

"I don't know, Honey. I'm not altogether certain it was for self-protection either."

"Do you think they recognized us?"

"No, I don't think so. At least I hope not."

Embry's hands were still shaking and she was barely doing the speed limit when a car came up behind them out of nowhere. She thought they were passing when instead, the car pulled up next to them and matched their speed. "Mom! Mom! They caught up to us."

Willow looked over and Preston was behind the wheel. "Embry, pull over."

"What? Are you crazy?"

"I said pull over. This is going to stop."

Embry brought her car to stop and just stared straight ahead. "We're going to die. I'm never going to fall in love. I'm never going to get married. I'm not going to have kids." She looked at Willow who was already half way out of the car. "Do you think Marshall will come to my funeral?"

"You're not going to die. At least not today." Willow shut the door and marched over to Preston's car. "What do you think you're doing? You nearly scared Embry to death. I could pummel you. That is my daughter you're messing with."

Preston opened his mouth to speak but the words didn't come.

"What do you have to say for yourself? Did you mean to scare the snot out of my daughter? Did you want her to drive off the road and flip her car and kill the both of us? Is that what you wanted?"

"I…I…didn't know it was you. I swear. I got a call that we had some women trespassing and they gave me a description of the car. I saw you turn and decided to follow…I didn't mean anything by it, I promise."

"I should hope not. We're going home now. And tell your guard, or whoever he is, if he ever points a gun at me or my daughter again he'll wish he had never lived."

Willow marched to her daughter's door, opened it, then led Embry to the passenger side and tucked her safely in. She took Embry's place and left a speechless Preston to wonder exactly what had just happened.

# Chapter 15

Willow paced, still dealing with what she had put her daughter through, as she waited for Steve. When the doorbell rang, she nearly jumped out of her skin. Clover's bark gave her a little bit of peace of mind. If anyone was truly after her, at least they knew they would have a loud obnoxious dog to deal with. She looked out the peephole. "Steve." She flung open the door and threw herself in his arms and started sobbing. "I almost killed her. They were chasing us with guns. Embry was driving and they nearly ran us off the road."

"Woah, slow down, what are you talking about?" He held her close still to comfort her before pulling apart so he could see her face.

Between blowing her nose a thousand times and the off and on again crying it took nearly an hour to get the whole story out.

"So, Preston has armed guards and most likely illegals working in his watermelon fields?"

"Yes, you should have seen them. They were so scared, Steve. They didn't know what to do. They didn't know if we were there to arrest them or kill them…or what we were doing there. They didn't know what to think. Before the guards came for us I tried some of the numbers from Dean's call list. It was them. He was trying to call the workers. I don't know why."

"Things are starting to make sense. But I have to ask, what were you thinking? Why did you follow Brian?"

She hiccupped. "I thought he would have answers. He seemed the most likely, the shadiest. I still think he's to blame."

"There's no doubt he has his hand in the pot so to speak. But to what degree and how hot is the water? That is what I want to know." He tipped her chin. "These are dangerous men, Willow."

"I didn't think they would do us any harm. I just thought maybe we could find something out."

"Willow, if Preston is capable of killing his nephew and Brian his best friend, what would keep them from hurting you and Embry?"

She started crying all over again.

He gently held her. "Where is Embry?"

"She's sleeping in my bed. I doubt she'll be able to go home tonight. She might even need counseling. There goes her inheritance." The waterworks started once again.

Steve was thankful Willow couldn't see his smile. "Oh, I don't think it'll come to that. We need to figure out how we can catch whoever is responsible red handed."

"Oh…Preston asked Brian to handle an incoming shipment that's due in tomorrow. Do you think that it's something illegal? Maybe drugs?"

"I have my guesses. For now, why don't I make you two something to eat and sit here with you for a while? Embry isn't the only one who needs comforting."

Steve set about making the only thing he knew he could do well—omelets. He found everything he needed in Willow's refrigerator while she went to check on Embry.

The smell of bacon sizzling brought both of them out of Willow's bedroom.

Embry smiled and gave Steve a hug. "I'm really fine. It got a little scary. I thought I was going to die, but, overall, I had fun."

He shook his head. "Both of you, sit down."

He placed plates before them then carried his own to the table and joined them. "Bon appetit." He bowed his head for a few seconds then dug in.

## This Little Piggy Wound Up Dead

When all three finished their meal, Embry asked what each one was thinking. "What now?"

Steve wiped his mouth with his napkin then said, "I think today proves you both need to let this go and let the police do their jobs."

Embry looked from her mother to Steve then back again. "Mom? The police have the wrong person. Are we okay with that?"

Willow sighed. On one hand, she didn't want to do anything to jeopardize the well-being of her daughter. On the other hand, they really did have the wrong guy. Yeah, maybe Chester needed a swift kick in the pants but he didn't commit murder. She was now 100% certain of it. "Honey, more than anything I want you safe."

"So, that's it then? The most important thing is us? What happened to everything you've taught me in life? To give and think of others? To do what's right? So, as long as I'm safe all that thinking is good but if there's any risk at all—forget it? I'm sorry, but I can't do that."

She got up and stomped to the back bedroom.

Willow sighed. "She's right, ya know? I didn't raise her to quit when things got tough. That's not the way we do things."

Steve moved his chair closer to Willow. "Willow, you know what they're capable of. Dean is dead. So is Bridget. Whatever's driving these people is worth killing over. I don't want anything to happen to you. To either of you." He gently touched her face. "I've just found you. I don't want to lose you."

Willow felt her eyes gloss over. It had been a long time since anyone spoke to her in such a way. She blinked away the tears. "I wouldn't be me if I didn't stand by my convictions. I admit, I was hoping you could convince Embry to drop the whole thing, go home, have a good cry and then get on with life. But once she was safe, I had every intention of finding the murderer. I wasn't going to let this go."

He tilted her chin up. "You wouldn't be the Willow I've come to…"

He was interrupted by Embry who marched out of the back bedroom with her backpack and purse. "I'm leaving. If you two aren't going to do what's right, I will by myself."

Willow jumped up. "Hey, whoa. Slow down. Who said we're not doing anything?"

"Well..." She hiccuped. "…you didn't say you were going to."

"Embry, you didn't give me time. We've been sitting here talking about what we should do while you've been back there getting mad. You could come sit down and help us figure it out?"

## This Little Piggy Wound Up Dead

Embry blew her nose. "Are you sure you're going to do something?"

Willow hugged her. "You know me better than that." She pulled back. "I just wanted to protect you. You're my baby."

Steve stepped up to the two women. "I want to protect both of you. It's how God made me. Nothing will ever change that."

Embry pulled Steve into their hug. "You look like you could use one."

He sniffed then smiled. "Yeah, I was kind of feeling left out."

The three of them spent the rest of the evening figuring out exactly how they were going to bring Dean and Bridget's murderer to justice.

# Chapter 16

Embry didn't hear enough of Brian and Preston's conversation to know what time or where the meeting was going down so it was another early morning for Willow. Much to her chagrin. The only bright spot, besides hopefully catching a murderer that is, was having someone cook for you—the second day in a row. This time it was Embry at the stove. Willow sat back. Her daughter had somehow grown up on her. *When did that happen?*

"It's almost ready." She glanced at the clock. "Where is Steve?"

"I don't know. He should have been here by now." She glanced at her phone. No updates. "Well, I guess we eat without him. Something must have come up."

Embry dished out the skillet scramble she had whipped together. "Do you think he changed his mind?"

"Nope. I don't. He knows this is important to both of us. Besides, I think he knows better to pull something like that." She closed her eyes and sniffed the combination of eggs, Brussel sprouts, Canadian bacon, spinach, and cheese. She buttered her bagel. "Today's the day, I can feel it." She took a bite and scowled at Clover, who was lying at her feet hoping for an accident. "Go lay down." She pointed to the living area. The dog begrudgingly went just behind the dividing line and lay down with her nose mere millimeters from the "dining" area. Willow just shook her head.

Just as Embry sat down the doorbell rang. Clover jumped up and ran for the door. Willow followed. "Clover, you're lying down on duty. What happened girl? Did breakfast distract you?"

Willow opened the door for Steve. "Come on in. You almost missed breakfast."

"Sorry I'm late. It couldn't be helped." He scooped up some of the egg mixture on his plate, careful to leave the Brussel sprouts in the pan. "Looks delicious. Thanks!"

Willow glanced over his shoulder and grinned. "Oh, man, looks like you didn't get any Brussel sprouts. I'll get you some."

He pulled his plate away from the stove and hurried to the table. "Oh no, I want to make sure there's plenty for you two." He popped a fork full in his mouth. "Mm…this is good. I've never had eggs this way."

Willow poured him a cup of coffee and put a bagel down for him. "So, what held you up?"

"Just digging up information on our friends Brian and Preston. For instance…" he ate a quick bite. "…did you know that Preston owns a straight box truck?"

Both Willow and Embry shook their heads.

Steve continued. "What do you suppose he uses that for? And why were there armed guards in Preston's field? It certainly wasn't to protect anyone. Maybe protect an investment. Certainly not people." He scraped the remainder of the eggs off his plate.

Embry asked, "What are you thinking?"

Willow handed him his bagel. "Do you want more eggs?"

He raised his eyebrows. "You don't mind?" He addressed Embry's question as Willow refilled his plate. "I'm thinking there are illegal activities happening at Preston's farm. I also happen to know today is the watermelon festival in Rush Springs. We may just catch us a killer if we get moving."

Steve watched Willow put the remainder of the eggs in Clover's dish. "You're not supposed to give her people food. It's not good for her."

"But, she loves it. Look at those puppy dog eyes. Besides, our vet said eggs are great for dogs."

## This Little Piggy Wound Up Dead

Steve gave her a look. "Did he also say cheeseburgers are good for her?"

"Hush. We have to hurry, remember?"

Willow's jeep pulled into Rush Springs. "Wow. It's packed." She glanced at her watch. "And it's only 10. Where did all these people come from?"

He pretended offence and grabbed his heart. "The watermelon festival is nationally famous. We happen to have the best watermelon crop in the nation. Just wait till you taste it."

"How can you even think of food with all you ate for breakfast?"

He rubbed his stomach. "Oh, I think I'll manage. Let's find a good stand to purchase one. I know the perfect one." He pointed to a trailer laden with watermelons. "That one looks good. Pull over and let's get us a watermelon."

The three wandered to the flatbed where a few Hispanic people were standing around with Preston keeping watch. "Well, look who the cat drug in. Fancy meetin' you here. I'm surprised you're not taking a walk out in the country, smelling the fresh country air."

Willow noticed he added that little bit for her benefit. She felt the anger rise up and she mentally suppressed it. *No time for that right now. I've gotta get information from him.*

"Nope, not today. We're here for the festival and to get some watermelon. I've heard rave reviews." Well, technically, the only review was from Steve. Still yet, he did rave.

"I've got some cut up." He handed the three of them a piece. "Have a taste."

Willow had to admit, the watermelon was the best she'd ever had. "I'll take two."

The young lady, probably younger than Embry, who helped her load the watermelon was incredibly beautiful. She carried one of the watermelons to the truck while Willow had the other. Steve had started to take the watermelon, but the girl shook her head. She set the watermelon carefully on the back seat while Steve kept Preston occupied. The girl barely whispered, "Por favor, ayúdame." Willow vowed she was going to learn Spanish. She repeated the phrase to herself a few times until she reached Embry. Por favor was easy. It was the word following por favor that was throwing her for a loop.

The girl stood quietly with her eyes downcast while she waited to help the next customer. Willow couldn't help but stare.

Preston noticed Willow's person of interest. "She doesn't speak a word of English. My foreman's niece. Just came from Mexico. She'll be heading home soon. Just here for a visit." He addressed the girl harshly, although quietly, in Spanish. "callate la boca"

Embry kept a cool head and didn't let on that she could understand what was being said although her heart was breaking for the girl. She was obviously scared out of her mind. After experiencing a small dose of his wrath, Embry could completely understand.

Saying she had to use the facilities, Willow finally said goodbye. Getting older had its perks. She wasn't lying. She really did have to go. They found a small café on Main Street that had sandwiches for sale. While Steve bought them each one to go, Willow made use of the bathroom. Afterward, she told Embry and Steve what the girl had whispered to her.

Both Embry and Steve spoke at the same time. "Please help me."

Willow's eyes grew wide. "Steve, there's something sinister about that man."

Steve nodded. "That he is." His phone rang and after a brief conversation, he said, "Ladies, I know you both want to walk through the rest of the festival but we have a date with a truck. My guys found it. You ready?"

# Chapter 17

Steve pulled up behind the cruiser that pulled the truck over. No one was moving. "You two stay right here. Do not, I repeat, do not get out of this truck."

He exited Willow's Jeep and walked to the cruiser. "Good job. Any trouble so far?"

The officer nodded his head. "Not a peep."

Steve approached the driver's side door, showed his badge, and asked the driver for his driver's license and registration. If the situation wasn't so serious he would have started laughing. Elvis was driving. "Sir, I'm going to have to ask you to step out of the truck."

"Is there a problem, Officer?"

"I don't know yet. That is what we're going to find out."

The man opened the truck door and slipped out of the driver's seat. He stood next to the truck and if he was doing anything illegal, he sure didn't seem nervous.

Willow rolled down their windows so they could hear as Steve interacted with the driver.

"Sir, we have a warrant to search your truck. I need you to open the back, please."

"Well, we're gonna have a problem then. I don't have a key to the back. I just drive. No one tells me what I'm moving."

Steve nodded to the police officer who took a large pair of bolt cutters and cut the padlock on the back of the truck. He lifted the door and everyone gasped. Hispanic families were huddled together. The inside of the truck smelled like human waste.

Willow wasted no time. She jumped out of her vehicle and joined Steve. Embry was right behind her.

"I told you…" He stopped speaking. The tears in her eyes convinced him there would be no stopping this woman from helping these people. There were children ranging in age from toddlers to teenagers. Men and woman held onto children who were so fatigued and dehydrated, Steve was afraid some of them were dead. He prayed that was not the case.

He called for backup and ambulances. He couldn't say this surprised him. The armed guards on Preston's farm were to keep people in, not from coming in. The uniformed officer cuffed the driver.

## This Little Piggy Wound Up Dead

Willow went to her truck and returned with a full case of water. "I keep it there for emergencies. I'd say this classifies." She and Embry were helping families down from the truck and handing out water, which they cautioned the recipients to drink slowly.

The last of the families were unloaded as the EMT's arrived. Willow started counting. "Steve, there's got to be at least 50 people here. Why would he do this? Who treats people this way?"

Steve shook his head in disgust and answered her questions. "Preston does and it's all for money."

"How does doing this make him money?"

"Well, to start with, free labor. Remember the workers you were calling? The ones whose phones were ringing? Most likely they're paying off a debt. Or the rest of a debt. It costs thousands of dollars to sneak across the border. He gets workers for pennies on the dollar. Cheap labor. And then of course there are the ones who pay up front. He has a thriving business. And it's not growing watermelon."

"But, that's slavery."

"Yep. It sure is. And these families are so desperate they will do whatever it takes to get to America. Mexico is a dangerous place. Here, they can live the American dream. They can live in relative safety, work hard, and make a living without worrying about their children being kidnapped."

Willow began to respond then noticed a nice shiny red Mercedes pass slowly by. "Steve, it's Brian. This is what he was supposed to do for Preston. This was the delivery he was supposed to meet."

As Steve made eye contact with Brian he gunned his car. Steve called in a B.O.L.O. alert on Brian. It was only a matter of time before he was picked up. There weren't too many places he could hide. Steve also sent a squad car to the festival to pick up Preston. The Oklahoma City Police Department was anxiously awaiting their arrival.

# Chapter 18

The ambulances took the families to be checked out. Willow wasn't sure what would happen to them. Certainly they crossed the border illegally. If only they could go through the right channels and come here legally. Maybe then they wouldn't have to put theirs and their children's lives in danger. Her heart broke for them. She was so thankful she never had to make such a choice.

Steve caught a ride with the police officer who was on the scene. Willow was worried about the young girl they met at the watermelon stand. Certainly Preston was already in custody. She couldn't imagine she and Embry would be in any danger if they tried to find the girl.

The watermelon stand was still operating although the girl wasn't anywhere in sight. When Embry asked for her, all she received in response were shrugs. No one seemed to know where she was.

"Let's go to Preston's farm. Maybe she's there."

The women drove around the block first. Everything seemed peaceful, calm. There were no workers in the fields and from what they could see, no guards with guns. In fact, the farm looked like a ghost town.

Willow drove down the long drive way. The gate was open so why not? She parked in front of the house. Both sat quietly, waiting. No greeting committee showed up bearing arms.

They began to walk around the farm. Surely someone was about, not everyone would be gone.

First they looked through the house windows into what appeared to be the living room. Nothing seemed out of place.

Willow watched her daughter start for the opposite side of the house. "Stick close. I don't want to separate."

Embry nodded then followed her mother. As they rounded the corner of the house they both saw movement. Or at least they thought they did.

"Did you see that too?" Embry looked in the direction the blur went. "Or am I crazy?"

"No, I think I saw it too. The only problem is, I'm not sure what it is."

The two women walked in the direction of the out buildings. As they drew closer, they heard whimpering. Embry whispered. "Sounds like someone crying."

## This Little Piggy Wound Up Dead

Willow removed her Taser from her pocket and held her finger to her lips. The crying grew louder as they approached the barn door. Willow slipped around the door first, putting herself between her daughter and danger.

Her heart broke as she saw the beautiful young woman from the watermelon festival all alone, sobbing. She sat down beside her on a bale of hay. "What is the matter? What happened."

"Mi familia. They are gone."

"You speak English!" Willow was astonished. "Why didn't you use English earlier? And what do you mean your family is gone?"

"He could not hear me. He did not know I speak English. It was better that way." She stood. "Come, I show you." She led Willow and Embry to an open door with a padlock hanging from it. "See, they are gone."

Willow looked around the cramped room. A few pieces of clothing and a few blankets were scattered around the room. A child's doll was propped up against the wall. All other traces of human occupancy were gone. She turned to the young lady. "What is your name?"

"Adelina."

"Adelina, where did they go?"

"I do not know, senorita. I only know if I do not do as they say, they will hurt mi familia."

She looked down in shame. "I have to do what they say. I love mi familia."

Willow led the young woman to her truck. "We're going to find your family. I have a friend who is a police officer…"

The long legged beauty backed away from Willow's vehicle. "I cannot go to la policia."

Embry reached out to her. "The police here are different than in Mexico. It's okay. You'll be safe."

"No, Mr. Preston say the policia will send my familia to jail. And me. I cannot go to them."

Embry tried again. "Adelina, we will help you. Please, come with us. You have to trust us." She looked around. "What else are you going to do?"

With this question, Adelina started crying once again. "I do not know what to do. I do not like Mr. Preston but at least I have food to eat." She hesitated then added. "And a place to sleep." The last of her statement caused her face to turn red.

Willow and Embry looked at one other, questioning one another silently as to whether or not they should say anything.

"Adelina, how old are your parents?"

"Why do you ask, Senorita?"

## This Little Piggy Wound Up Dead

"If we are going to help you find them we need to know about them."

"Why are you trying to find my parents?"

Willow pointed toward Embry. "We told you we would help you find them."

"Ah, Senorita, my parents are in Mexico. I know where my parents are. I am missing mi esposa and mi hija. They were in this room. Now they are gone."

Willow's mouth dropped in shock. Yes, the girl was beautiful. Did Preston take a married woman from her husband—just so he could have her? The idea made her sick to her stomach. When she thought Adelina was a single young woman she could have wrapped her hands around his neck and wrung it. She didn't want to think about what she could do with this new information.

"Adelina, is there any place that Preston might have taken them? Can you think of anything?"

Embry had disappeared while Willow was talking with Adelina. A little while later, she reappeared. "Mom, you're gonna want to see this." She led them to another building and opened the locked door. Crammed inside were around a hundred Hispanic men, women, and children. Everyone silently stared. Fear marked some of their faces. Resigned defeat others'.

Adelina gasped. "Pedro, Felicia!" She ran to a handsome man holding a toddler girl in the middle of the crowd then turned to Willow and Embry.

"What happens to us now, Senoritas?"

# Chapter 19

Willow found the back door open to the kitchen. She found eggs, cheese, and tortillas in the refrigerator, cans of refried beans in the pantry, and sausage in the deep freeze. After calling Steve and telling him who they found, she and Embry got to work making lunch for the crowd. It wasn't gourmet but she doubted they would complain. They looked hungry, thirsty, and hot. That metal building could have been their coffin. She shuddered.

The ladies were filling pitchers with water and the husbands and children were drinking greedily. She whispered to Embry. "Are they all here illegally?"

Embry nodded. "Most likely. They wouldn't be in this situation otherwise."

"How did they get here? I mean, I know some people cross on foot but surely not the children."

Embry stopped what she was doing and stared. "Mom, how do you think they got here?"

"I don't know. I mean, why would they take their children on such a dangerous trip? Why didn't they just stay in Mexico or wherever they were living?"

Steve walked in dressed as a civilian in the middle of their discussion and answered Willow's question. "Because the dream of giving their children a safe place to grow up far outweighs the possible danger from the crossing. And many people make it safely and live undiscovered for many years. What we need to do is give these people a better way to come legally."

Adelina's husband stepped forward. "Sir, My name is Pedro Lorenzo Garcia Cardenas."

Steve, Willow, and Embry waited for him to go on. Upon seeing their expressions, Pedro continued. "My family and I are here legally. We have been granted political asylum from the United States government."

"If you are here legally, why did you cross the border in such a manner?"

"For safety reasons. If we have come by more, how do you say…conventional methods, yes, then surely we would not have made it. Very dangerous men are looking for us. My position with the government made me a target with many drug dealers and many crooked politicians." He rattled off his lawyer's name and phone number.

"Please call him. He will verify this information and come for me and my family."

Steve wrote down the information while Willow, Embry, and a few of the ladies finished preparing and serving the meal. Once fed, the children began to perk up and sound like children again. The adults spoke quietly among themselves.

Willow was concerned. "What is going to happen to them?"

"They'll be sent back. And many of them will do this all over again. Even with what they went through, to them, it's worth it."

"There has to be a better way."

Steve made the phone call and sure enough, Pedro was telling the truth. His father was an official in Mexico City who had gone after the drug cartels. He was abducted and killed and then strung up as an example for anyone else who thought they would follow his example, including his young son. The government itself began targeting Pedro as he grew older and started speaking out against what was going on in their country. When that happened, he sought protection for his family. Because so many were corrupt, he temporarily changed his name and travelled as a commoner who wanted freedom in the United States. Unfortunately, he connected with a coyote who had affiliations with a corrupt man in the United States, Preston Mosely.

A driver came to pick up Pedro and Adelina and their young daughter. Shortly thereafter, the rest of the refugees were taken for processing. Steve followed Willow and Embry back to the ice cream shop where they all sat down with a hot cup of coffee.

Embry added a plate of layered brownies and lemon bars to the middle of the table. "I'm starving."

Willow, for the moment, ignored the food. "Were Brian and Preston caught? I've got to know."

Steve grinned. "Yep, and Brian gave up everything. Seems as though Preston had made him and Dean a deal they couldn't refuse. They were the transportation behind the operation. More money than either of them could handle. Dean, well, he spent about all his money on drugs and women and just rough living. Brian bought social status. Then one day Dean develops a conscience. His money was gone so he stole 50 thousand from his uncle and redistributed the money to the illegals they had brought across.

## This Little Piggy Wound Up Dead

Preston couldn't exactly go to the police with his story therefore he concocted his phony savings plan for the food truck—which had been his dream in his younger years—and apparently being the good uncle he forgave his nephew. Which was a crock of baloney. Preston assigned the dirty work of dealing with his stealing nephew to his hired muscle and went to bed the night of the BBQ contest knowing his problem would be taken care of. When he woke up, he truly was surprised to see him tied up in the smoker. He expected him to be dead, yes, but in the smoker? That threw him."

Embry asked, "So, Preston killed his own nephew, over money?"

Steve nodded. "He sure did."

"What about Brian, what was his part in all this?" Willow mumbled as she took a bite.

"Brian was trying to talk Dean into going to Preston and apologizing. He knew his uncle would call off the hit if he agreed to work off his debt and then some. Dean had refused. Brian was going to try one last time and had agreed to meet him near to where he was killed. Well, when Brian arrived, Dean was already dead. He'd been beaten pretty bad and then stabbed. So he took off and went back to his camp. He figured since he didn't touch anything he wouldn't be placed at the scene of the crime.

"The police were still trying to figure out how he ended up in the smoker so they went back to the kids from the baseball team. It appears Chester wasn't the only one to go back to check on Dean. A few of the more notorious players went back to finish him off and found him dead so they tied him up like—and I quote—the pig he was and stuck him in the smoker."

"What about Bridget? Why did they murder her?"

Steve grimaced. "Seems Brian told her what happened and she threatened to go to the police. I guess after you've killed once the second time around isn't so hard."

Willow shook her head in disgust. "I guess not."

"Dean had his hands involved in way too many bad situations for this to have been easy." He smiled at Willow. "Too bad for the lot of them you happened to be walking through the park when you did. Well, for all but Chester. The rest may have gotten away with it and Chester would have taken the blame. Chester is still being held but at least he's not going up for murder. What a convoluted mess!"

# This Little Piggy Wound Up Dead

Willow twirled her hair. "So that is how the pig came to rest in the smoker."

# Chapter 20

Willow lit the candles and slid down into the hot bath water. She was exhausted and looking forward to the next morning. She still needed to wash and dye her hair. With all the sleuthing she'd missed her hair appointment. She held her hands up. "I guess they'll have to do." She awoke with a start as Clover licked her hand as it hung over the edge of the tub.

"Girl, you're a lifesaver. I could have slept in their all night." She toweled off and applied lotion. Not something she did often, although she should have. Her skin absorbed the healing balm and thanked her for the attention.

She let the dog out then slid beneath the covers for a long overdue good night's sleep.

The next morning she did a quick touch up on her roots and scrubbed her fingernails really well. *Perhaps I'll have time between the gun show and the fundraiser for a quick manicure.* She slipped on a pair of jeans and ran to meet Steve's truck.

She opened the door before he could get out. "Hey." She jumped in and buckled her belt.

I'm excited. I've decided I need something small, unobtrusive. Something that will be easy to reach for and do some damage if I need it to."

"I have just the gun in mind."

Together they walked the gun show floor looking at all the different options. Steve stopped at nearly every table. Between the guns, knives, archery equipment and, well, all the other "guy" stuff, she could understand the draw. Finally he shook hands with a vendor. "Willow, this is Troy. A friend from high school. Troy, this is the gal I was telling you about."

Troy nodded and then pulled a gun from under the table and handed it to Steve. "Good to meet you, Willow."

Steve looked the gun over then handed it to Willow. "How does this feel?"

Willow passed the gun from hand to hand then placed her hand over the handle. It fit perfectly in her grip.

"Do you like it?"

She nodded. "I really don't know too much about them. If this one is the best one for what I need, then I'm good with it."

"I'm assuming you're going to be concealing?" Troy removed a holster from his case.

She looked to Steve who answered for her. "Yeah, once she gets licensed. She's starting classes next week."

"Good to hear. Steve won't let you get into any trouble. He'll make sure everything gets done by the book."

An hour later Willow was the proud owner of her first handgun. She had a few cartridges, the holster, a cleaning kit, and a case. Steve dropped her off with the promise to be back to pick her up in a few hours.

She glanced at her watch then called to see if she could get a quick manicure in town. Thankfully, they had an opening. A simple manicure would do the trick. An hour later, her hands looked much better. She styled her hair and applied the new makeup Embry had insisted on her buying after being mistaken for a homeless woman. She turned her face from side to side as she looked in the mirror. "If I must say so myself, not too bad."

The black dress glided over her shoulders and swished as it fell. The lotion she'd applied the evening before had done its job and softened her rough exterior.

Last to be applied was a dab of perfume. Just enough to capture his senses. Not enough to overpower and offend anyone else. She had switched out her purse and now carried a little case only big enough for her id and a tube of lipstick. Thankfully Steve would be with her and she'd have no need for her Taser.

Her pantyhose did a suitable job of covering up her sore toe. Her heels were wide enough so as not to pinch the toe either.

She opened the front door to the most handsome man she'd ever laid eyes on. He was in a black tux and his shoes shined. His hair was perfectly groomed and his smile, well, his smile never changed. She held the door open wide for him to come in but he seemed rooted in that spot. "Steve, you coming in?"

He opened his mouth but words did not come. He tried again. "Willow…" He swallowed hard. "…you're absolutely stunning. You're beautiful."

She smiled as he helped her with her light sweater.

"We're traveling in class this evening."

He held open the car door. "Yeah, my sister insisted I take one of their cars. They both drive Cadillac's."

Willow had always drove more rugged vehicles so this was her first encounter with luxury. "I could get used to this." She ran her hand over the plush temperature controlled seat.

Steve sat next to her and once again found himself staring. He'd always found her beautiful. Her wit and charm, her sense of humor and her adoration and devotion to her daughter just added to her beauty. Tonight, seeing her in her finery and looking like she just stepped off a Paris runway, was enough to take his breath away. He barely said a word the entire drive. "So could I."

"So could I what?"

He looked at her with confusion. "Get used to this."

She laughed. "Oh, it's nice isn't it?"

He shook his head. He didn't care about the car. The lady sitting next to him was what he could get used to.

Willow watched as Steve gave his sister a kiss on the cheek. "Wow, Bro. You clean up nice."

He smiled. "You don't look so bad yourself."

Willow gaped. His sister was drop dead gorgeous. Not so bad? *Standing next to her I'd be labeled as plain.*

Willow gave her a hug. "It's good to see you again."

"You too! How is Clover doing?"

They spent the next few minutes talking about the antics of her dog while the guys found them something to drink.

## This Little Piggy Wound Up Dead

Willow found herself being stared at all the way through dinner. Every time she returned his gaze, he would quickly look away. She felt her face flushing.

The waiters removed their dinnerware and announced the orchestra would be starting shortly. Steve stood then reached for Willow's hand. "Would you like to walk in the gardens?"

She took his hand and nodded. Together they walked through the twinkling candlelight. The scent of roses was heavy and the night sky was filled with stars. She glanced heavenward and rubbed her arms.

"Are you cold?" He draped her sweater over her shoulders then wrapped his arm around her. "If this doesn't warm you up, I'll give you my jacket.

She wanted to tell him she wasn't cold. It wasn't the evening air that was giving her goosebumps. It was being so close to him. It was his touch. Neither a sweater nor a jacket would cure her. "I'm fine, really." *Woman, kiss him already!* She mentally chastised herself. She wanted to wrap her arms around his neck and press her lips to his but she knew he was a gentleman. So, she waited.

"Look at the moon." He pointed upward.

"It's so big…so beautiful." She managed to take her eyes from the pull of the moon and look to Steve who was once again staring.

"I'm sorry. It's just…" Steve could hear the violins in the background. He took both her hands. The cellos joined the serenade. He pulled her closer. The trumpets came in loud and strong followed by the kettle drums. He could stand it no longer. He pulled her to him and just as the music reached an all-time high he pressed his lips to hers.

They both savored the kiss. When Steve finally pulled away, he brushed her lips with his thumb. He whispered in her ear. "I'm sorry for staring. But tonight, I see nothing else worth looking at." He lifted her chin and kissed her once more. This time, neither heard the music. There was nothing but them.

# Willow's Lemon Bars

½ cup butter
¼ cup powdered sugar
1 cup flour
½ tsp baking powder
2 eggs
1 cup granulated sugar
Zest of ½ lemon
2 tbsp. flour
2 tbsp. lemon juice

Preheat oven to 350 degrees. Butter sides of an 8x8 glass pan.

Cream butter. Add powdered sugar, baking powder, and flour. Press into bottom of baking dish. Bake for 20 minutes. Combine eggs, granulated sugar, lemon zest, 2 Tbsps flour, and lemon juice. Pour over baked crust and bake an additional 20-25 minutes at 350 degrees. Remove from oven. Cool and sift powdered sugar over lemon filling. Cut into squares and enjoy.

# Willow's Layered Brownies

Preheat oven to 350 degrees
Grease 9x13 glass pan

2 cups sugar
1 ½ cups flour
¾ cup baking cocoa
½ tsp salt
1 cup vegetable oil
4 eggs
2 tsp. vanilla
½ cup chopped pecans
½ cup chocolate chips

(or use your favorite boxed mix to make things easier…but be sure to add those pecans and chocolate chips)

14 ounce bag caramels
14 ounce can sweetened condensed milk
½ cup chopped pecans

## This Little Piggy Wound Up Dead

Mix first set of ingredients and add half of mixture to a prepared 9x13 pan. Bake at 350 degrees for 10 minutes. Melt caramel and sweetened condensed milk in medium saucepan over low heat. Add pecans and spread over baked brownie mixture. Spread remainder brownie batter over caramel and bake for an additional 20 to 25 minutes, depending on how gooey you like your brownies.

Cool brownies.

Beat the following ingredients and spread on cooled brownies:

    ½ cup butter
    ½ cup brown sugar, packed
    ¼ cup sugar
    2 tbsp. milk
    1 tsp. vanilla
    1 cup flour

Refrigerate to set filling. Once chilled,

Melt 2 cups of chocolate chips and 1 tbsp. shortening. Spread on chilled brownies and top with whole pecans. Cool. Cut into squares and serve.

# Willow's Chicken Enchiladas

*(Notice dessert came first)*

2 pounds chicken breast, cut into cubes
Grapeseed oil
1 medium onion, chopped
1 4 ounce can green chilies
1 can cream of chicken soup
½ cup milk
1 cup sour cream
1 tsp chili powder
½ tsp garlic powder
3 cups Monterey Jack cheese
8 medium flour tortillas, cut into pieces (kitchen shears are great for this)

Grease 9x13 pan well. Layer bottom with ½ flour tortillas.

In a large fry pan sauté chicken in 3 tbsp. grapeseed oil. Add chopped onion and cook for 3 additional minutes until onions are translucent. Add green chilies, cream of chicken soup, milk, sour cream, chili powder, and garlic powder to pan. Continue cooking until sauce is blended, approximately 3-4 minutes. Ladle filling onto flour tortillas in 9x13 pan. Add two cups Monterey Jack cheese and remainder of flour tortillas to the pan. Bake at 350 degrees for 30 minutes until sauce is bubbly. Remove from oven and top with remaining cheese. Bake an additional two minutes until cheese is melted. Cut into squares and serve with chopped green onions and sour cream (optional).

# Willow's Marinade for grilled chicken

4 bone in chicken breasts
1 cup your favorite beer
¼ cup grapeseed oil
Juice from ½ lime
6 tbsp. BBQ Dry Rub from below

Combine all ingredients but chicken breasts. Set aside 1/3 cup of marinate to baste with. Place chicken breasts in a large zip lock bag with remaining marinade and refrigerate overnight.

Grill on hot grill for 12-15 minutes per side or until juices run clear. Baste often.

BBQ Dry Rub
1/3 cup cayenne pepper
1/3 cup chipotle pepper
2/3 cup paprika
2/3 cup garlic powder

# This Little Piggy Wound Up Dead

2/3 cup onion powder
1/3 cup seasoned salt
2/3 cup brown sugar
1/3 cup ground cumin

Mix all ingredients and store in cool place. Use as a dry rub for barbecuing or add to your favorite liquid marinade base.

# Please enjoy this excerpt from 'Southern Fried Son of a Gun', Book 4 of the Willow Crier Cozy Mystery Series

## Chapter 1

The heat seeking missile sat poised, ready to fire. She took aim. The target locked. She fired. The explosion rocked the intersection…

"Mom, hello, earth to mom."

Willow startled out of her daydream. "What?"

"What were you just doing?"

"Nothing."

"Mom, answer the question."

She pointed to the red pickup truck in front of them. "I just blew him up."

Embry raised her eye brows. "A little extreme, don't you think?"

## This Little Piggy Wound Up Dead

"He cut me off. I was in line first. I was being nice and I gave him room to get through. He didn't even acknowledge me. He had to go."

Embry shook her head. "Mom, I'm not sure you should have a gun. It might not be the wisest decision."

Willow patted her purse. "Oh, Honey, it's fine. Just because I want to rid the world of all the idiots doesn't mean I will."

Willow pulled into the parking space in front of a rather drab dirty brown building. "Are you ready?" Her gun club was meeting for a potluck. The concealed carry class Steve signed her up for got along so well they had decided to get together. Willow had decided food was the one way to get Embry to the club.

"Ready as I'll ever be. I guess." Embry opened her door. "Do I have to do this?"

"Yes. You do." She paused. "Well, I guess you don't. But if you ever want me to make homemade chicken potpie again you will."

"Mom, that's not fair."

"I don't play fair. Never claimed to either." Willow led the way to the front door and held it open for her daughter then followed her inside. The entry was a mini store and had glass cases with a few guns and some ammo. "You work downtown. Sometimes late at night. I've seen the kind of people who are wandering around at that time of night. I'll feel better knowing you can protect yourself." A deep southern voice ended their conversation.

"Willow, hey, how you doin', girl?" The elderly man looked to Embry. "Don't tell me. She's your sister, right?"

Willow grinned. "Flattery will get you everywhere. Clancy. This is my daughter, Embry. Embry, meet Clancy." She addressed Embry. "Clancy is a war hero."

"Girl, don't be goin' on about me. She don' wantta be hearin' no old war stories. She got better things to do than that."

Willow frowned. "Clancy, you should be proud of what you did. Not everyone would risk their own safety to help someone else. Especially if that someone else wasn't exactly friendly."

He waved her off. "Nah, anybody would have helped. I'm nothin' special." He went behind the counter and glanced at his watch. "You're a bit early for the potluck. What can I help you two ladies with today?"

Willow loved Clancy's range. It wasn't fancy like the others in town. It was a little off the beaten path and if you wanted a cup of coffee or a soda, your only choices were the vending machine or the crusty pot Clancy kept on the counter. Granted, the coffee would put hair on your chest but once you got used to it, it was almost like coming home. She smiled. "You got me. My dish is in the cooler in the Jeep. Since I was coming anyway, I thought I'd get some practice time in." She motioned to Embry. "She's never shot a gun. I want her to be able to protect herself. So, I'd like two lanes. And a rental for Embry."

Clancy nodded. "You got it." He pulled out a Smith & Wesson revolver and some ammo. "This should do the trick. Jason, can you give this young lady a rundown on the 1911?"

"Sure Mr. C." Jason put his duster behind the counter. "Which lane did you assign to her?"

"I put them in eight and nine. Maybe you can use the classroom and go over the rules and the gun."

Jason nodded, took the gun and the ammo, and walked away.

Embry gave her mom a look then shrugged and followed the young man with the buzz cut through a hallway and into a small classroom. Willow entered right behind them. A refresher course wouldn't hurt, nor would learning about another weapon. A half hour later Jason led both women to their lanes and got them each set up with a target. "Okay, why don't you give it a go and I'll stay here and help you out for a bit."

Embry loaded the weapon as she had been instructed then took aim and fired. She looked to Jason for input. He simply nodded so she fired again.

This time he interjected. "You need to keep both eyes open."

She nodded then fired again, making sure both eyes were fully open.

Jason motioned for her to set her weapon down and he brought the target forward. Two shots were off the paper to the right of the silhouette. One was in the chest. "See what happens when you are aware of your target? You hit it." He sent a clean target out. "Let's try it again."

She spent her round of ammunition and then drew in the target. Every shot was a hit. Not all were kill shots, but she did have a couple. As much as she didn't want to like firing the weapon, she had to admit, it felt good. Jason seemed impressed as well.

"You're good at this. How long have you been target shooting?"

"This is my first time."

"You're kidding? I never would have guessed." After watching her load her weapon he excused himself. "If you need anything just give me a yell."

## This Little Piggy Wound Up Dead

Willow watched as Embry put her earplugs in and joined her in warding off various criminals. All put out of their misery, of course. She knew her daughter would be a natural. It would have to run in the family.

Shortly before their time ran out on the lane the lights flickered. Willow glanced around but nothing seemed out of the ordinary so she finished off her round and cleaned her gun as she waited for Embry to do the same.

"Well, what did you think?"

Embry's face lit up. "I loved it. I didn't think I would, but I did."

Willow laughed. "I knew you would."

Together they turned in Embry's weapon to Jason. "Clancy taking a break? He's joining us for the potluck, right?"

"Yeah. He's out back taking a smoke break." He rolled his eyes. "He'll be back in a few minutes."

Willow holstered her gun and went for her cooler. She made a broccoli salad and chocolate chip cookies. She also picked up a couple of gallons of sweet tea. Birdie pulled into the parking spot next to Willow's Jeep. She waved.

Birdie drank copious amounts of caffeine. She flitted from one thing to another. Willow wasn't sure how it was possible for her to hold a gun still enough to hit any target, let alone one about to cause her physical harm. Willow watched as she popped out of her boxy-looking car and started for the building. Suddenly, she turned around.

"Willow, so sorry. Didn't see you there." She approached Willow and took the two gallons of tea from her then turned for the building. Willow lifted the cooler and tried to catch up, to no avail, of course. By the time Willow entered the classroom everyone was thanking Birdie for remembering to bring something to drink. The woman continued on as if she didn't hear them. She neither accepted their thanks nor denied she brought the sweet drink. Willow had gotten used to her demeanor. Classic Birdie. Today, Willow chose to ignore it. She'd already blown up one vehicle and taken out an army of bad guys. The range was great for working off aggression. Birdie was safe, for today.

Willow placed her salad and cookies on the conference table. She noticed Embry was still talking with Jason and wondered what Marshall would think of that. "You two seem to have a lot to talk about."

Embry blushed. "Jason was telling me about Clancy's time in Vietnam."

So maybe everything is all right with Marshall then, good. I really like that young man. "Interesting, huh?"

"I'm not sure interesting is the right word. Makes me want to smack somebody."

Willow laughed. "You better be careful. Next thing you'll be blowing up trucks in intersections." She looked around. "Clancy's been gone a long time. Longer than normal. I wonder if he's okay."

Jason scoped out the room. "I'll go look out front. Maybe he had a customer come in."

More of her classmates filed into the room. Someone made fried chicken. Willow could smell it and looked down at her growling stomach. "Traitor." She had every intention to lose a few pounds. Funny how being in a new relationship did that to a girl.

She selected a breast from the glass pan and added her broccoli salad and a helping of fruit to her plate. Just as she and Embry sat down, Jason appeared looking as if he were going to be sick.

"Jason, what's wrong?" Willow scanned the room. "Where's Clancy."

He nodded then turned. Willow quickly followed him outside and around the building. She was thankful she hadn't taken a bite. If she had she would be losing it.

## Lilly York

A hot wire was hanging from the back of the building and Clancy was lying on the ground. The means of death was obvious. Someone fried their host. Clancy Cobb was electrocuted.

# Author Bio

Lilly York? (aka Darlene Shortridge, author of Contemporary Christian Fiction) How about Lilly Belle; a mis-plant northerner, living in a southern world. Southern charm is lost among late nights with a two year old granddaughter, heat flashes competing with hell, copious re-runs of Murder She Wrote with Jessica Fletcher catching the bad guy, and a vivid imagination keeping insanity at bay.

In both humor and mystery, Lilly draws inspiration from terrible twos, a 24 year old daughter who questions her sanity, a son who constantly spews bad puns, and a husband who has selective hearing. Though, that's perfectly alright with her, because what can you love more than a good laugh and a family so dysfunctional they almost seem functional?

To stay informed on the whereabouts and goings-on of the Willow Crier Cozy Mystery Characters as well as upcoming releases, recipes and maybe a clue or two, join Lilly's e-mail club by going to…

## LillyYork.com

# A Yankee's Guide to Southern Phrases

**Bless Your Heart**: The most back handed kind words spoken in the south. Means, while you're sweet, you're also stupid, you don't quite get it and I feel sorry for you.

**Fixin to**: About to do something, almost ready, thinking about doing something.

**Nervous as a long tail cat in a room full of rockin' chairs**: Nervous to the point of being jumpy.

**Reckon**: So suppose or believe something is true.

**Yankee**: Anyone originating north of the Mason Dixon line.

**Redneck**: Polite, blue collar individual who loves hunting, country music, and blue jeans. Add alcohol and anything can happen.

**Y'all**: You guys

## This Little Piggy Wound Up Dead

**All y'all**: More than five people

**I could eat the north end of a south-bound polecat**: Starving!

**Jerk a knot in your tail**: Typically used as a threat against someone as in, "If you do that again, I'm going to jerk a knot in your tail."

**Lil' Dogie**: A motherless calf, a calf separated from its cow.

**Hankering**: Craving something

**Fair to middlin'**: Doing okay

**Three sheets to the wind**: Drunker than a skunk

**Passel**: A whole bunch

**You ain't got no dog in this fight**: It's none of your business

CPSIA information can be obtained
at www.ICGtesting.com
Printed in the USA
LVHW080027060222
710380LV00022B/356